Billionaire Hero

Julie L. Spencer

Spencer Publishing, LLC

Click or scan here to request a complimentary book when you join my newsletter.

Copyright © 2021 by Julie L. Spencer

All rights reserved.

ISBN: 978-1-954666-00-9

www.AuthorJulieSpencer.com

Contents

Dedication

Billionaire Hero is dedicated to Tim Ballard and all the men and women who serve with him through the Operation Underground Railroad. Thank you for your service!

Prologue

Army Captain Monroe Cohen

"Why would any sane person want to jump out of a perfectly good airplane?" Monroe's dad used to say.

Yet here he stood—again—in full gear, heart racing, stomach tumbling, waiting for the final go-ahead. Not that Monroe wanted to jump; he was compelled to jump.

The United States flag sewn onto his uniform and the Special Forces insignia on the sleeve of his shoulder added the extra layer of necessity. Knowing the importance of the mission was the final driving force that gave him the courage to take that last step.

His team was counting on him. When he was given the green light, he leapt.

The rush of air pressed against his body as he plummeted toward the earth. So far below. Veiled in the black of night. Monroe could barely see what he knew was the canopy.

Monroe dove in the direction where his men were. They grasped one another's hands in a tight circle to keep themselves together. Then, with barely enough time to deploy their parachutes, they separated and silently slipped between the trees—and behind enemy lines.

Part One: Aaron's Story

As told by Prince Aaron Sayid, son of Prince Marcos Sayid, grandson of Prince Benjamin Sayid, great-grandson of Prince Marcos Sayid, great-great-grandson of King Sayid, who had recently passed away at the age of one hundred and six as the story begins...

Chapter One

Guatemala

Prince Aaron Sayid stepped out the door of the small airliner and into the Guatemalan sunshine. He slipped on a pair of black shades as he glanced around the tarmac, not really expecting to see Felicia but hoping nonetheless. He started down the stairs, followed by his younger brothers, Owen and Hayden.

The Mundo Maya-Flores International Airport was anything but international, unless the distance between Cancun, Mexico, and Flores, Guatemala, counted. Technically, the four-hour flight crossed over the border between the two countries, and that's what warranted the designation.

The princes rarely flew commercial. Although their family estate was worth over a billion dollars, they didn't want to wait for someone to charter a private jet. So they booked first-class seats on the earliest available flight and came to meet their feisty third cousin who was brave enough to reach out to them by telephone.

The Sayid brothers had lived in New York State all their lives even though they'd known they were heirs to the throne of the tiny Middle Eastern Kingdom of Madain Saleh. Their father, Prince Marcos Sayid, had served as Crown Prince until Aaron turned twenty, at which time the Crown had been conferred upon him during a simple coronation.

Aaron had claimed the title of Crown for just over a year before King Sayid died at the age of 106, and Aaron realized he didn't really want to move to the desert. He and his three younger brothers willingly abdicated the throne to one of their cousins who already lived in the kingdom.

Now they were merely spoiled, rich kids with time on their hands. Fly to Guatemala to meet a pretty girl? Sure, why not? What else would a twenty-one-year-old guy want to do for the summer?

Although they were royalty and Aaron and his brothers hadn't shown their faces on international television in several months, there was a small possibility of being recognized. They needn't have worried though. Three hot guys of Middle Eastern descent blended right in with the Hispanics in the tiny Guatemalan airport. All of them had thick, dark hair, caramel skin, and sultry, brown eyes.

They had arranged for a limo to take them to their hotel, so they expected to look for their names on a professional sign held by a driver.

Instead, a few friends and family members of other passengers held homemade signs. Among them was a petite ball of energy with long, black hair and a colorful dress that bounced along with her excitement. Her hand-drawn sign had Aaron's name spelled wrong and the 'S' backward.

Aaron knew the minute Felicia recognized him because she broke rank with the other people waiting and rushed forward, threw herself into his arms, and dropped her sign on the floor. Owen bent to pick up the sign as Aaron swung Felicia around, and they hugged as long-separated lovers would rather than two people meeting in person for the first time.

They'd texted and spent time together on video chat multiple times since she called him last week. He was introduced to her sisters and brothers and parents and best friends and her pet goat. He knew that her favorite breakfast was some sort of chocolate slop that he couldn't pronounce made from black beans and soaked up by homemade tortillas. He knew she was an expert at weaving and made textiles that the family sold at market. And he knew that she smelled like some sort of natural essential oil he could get lost in.

He closed his eyes and held her in the airport lobby while his brothers found their limo driver and waited for Aaron so they could retrieve their luggage.

"I have missed you," Felicia said in Spanish, her cheek pressed to his, her feet dangling around his knees, her arms around his neck. Although size was not indicative of age, combined with her youthful energy and excitement for life, she seemed too young to be twenty-one.

"We FaceTimed this morning," Aaron answered in Spanish, not releasing her from his arms. He'd taken a crash course refresher of his high school Spanish in preparation for this trip.

"That was many, many hours ago," she said, pulling back to look him in the eye.

He thought she was going to lean closer and kiss him, and he would have kissed her back without hesitation. Instead, she slid down, and he kept his hands on her waist until she regained her footing.

"Hola, Felicia," Hayden said, reaching for a hug. She hugged him but not with the same enthusiasm as she had Aaron. Then she reached over to hug Owen.

"Are you here alone?" Aaron glanced around for anyone else he might recognize from their video chats and found her father, Dominic Cohen, waiting nearby. Aaron was glad he hadn't kissed Felicia with her dad watching and stepped over with his hand extended. "Señor Cohen, good to meet you."

"Pleasure to meet you as well, Your Highness," Dominic said, shaking his hand and subtly bowing his head.

Aaron had grown up with the haughty attitude of royalty, and he was done with that. "Please, just call me Aaron," he said, also bowing subtly, bringing himself down to equal standing with the man who was his mother's cousin. "And these are my brothers, Hayden and Owen."

"Nice to meet you," Hayden said, shaking Dominic's hand.

"Thank you for welcoming us to your country," Owen said, also extending his hand to Dominic.

"How did you get to the airport? Do you have a car here in the city? Or would you like to ride back with us?" Aaron kept one arm around Felicia's waist as he spoke to her father. He couldn't seem to resist connecting with her now that they were together.

"We took a bus from Melchor de Mencos," Dominic said.

"You should ride with us in our limo." Aaron glanced around to find their waiting limo driver. "How much room do we have?"

"We have seating for eight, sir," the limo driver said. "But... your hotel is only ten minutes away."

"We could get a different hotel," Aaron said, turning back to Dominic. "Are there any hotels near your home?"

"There is one right in town," Dominic said, puffing out his chest proudly.

"Sir, my rates are quite high," the limo driver said in accented English, almost whispering, as if to give Aaron an opportunity to decline without embarrassing himself in front of his friends. "The fare would be much greater than taking the bus."

"How much?" Aaron asked in the same conspiratorial whisper, knowing the money didn't really matter.

"There and back, plus the gasoline, and my time, an hour and a half each way..." the limo driver, whose nametag read Joab, gave him a figure that was less than what Aaron had paid for a new suit to wear to his brother's graduation.

"I'll double that if you treat this lovely young lady as if she's a royal princess, and this gentleman"—he gestured to her father— "as if he's your honored guest," Aaron said, still whispering in English.

Joab pulled his shoulders back and lifted his chin. "Thank you, sir."

The man hurried to Felicia and held out his arm as he switched to Spanish and offered to escort her to the limousine.

"You sly dog," Hayden said with a chuckle.

"Uh, guys." Owen pulled them aside, showing them the screen of his phone. "The only hotel in Melchor de Mencos is a complete dive."

"Are there any others close?" Aaron asked.

Owen was already scrolling. "This one looks nice, and it's only twenty-five minutes farther. The San Ignacio Resort. Ooh, they have a suite called the Royal Suite. It's like the hotel knew we were coming."

"Ha, let me see that." Aaron took Owen's phone and strode over to where the driver was helping Felicia and Dominic into the limo. "Do you know where this hotel is located?"

"Yes, sir, but that's even farther." Joab's eyes grew wide.

"Would it help if I put you up in a room for the night?" Aaron asked.

"In *that* hotel?" The man looked as if he was holding a winning lottery ticket and wasn't sure if it was real. He seemed to catch himself and realize how his professional persona had slipped. Lifting his chin again, Joab said, "That would be acceptable."

"Perfect," Aaron said, then hurried over to climb into the car beside Felicia. He held the phone closer to her and Dominic to show them the website for the resort. "Look, we found something with more room and the hotel's only twenty-five minutes away from your house."

"But... that's in Belize." Felicia shrunk back and curled her lip.

"Is that okay?" Aaron wasn't sure what to think of her reaction.

"I'm sure it will be fine." Her voice squeaked at the end of her sentence as if she wasn't convinced.

Still, the resort seemed amazing from their website. He handed the phone back to Owen. "Book us a couple of rooms. And cancel our reservation here in Flores."

Felicia glanced at her father, then plastered on a fake smile. That's how they spent a very uncomfortable hour and a half on the way to their home.

Chapter Two

Tell Me Tomorrow

T he border town of Melchor de Mencos sat on the banks of the muddy Mopan River, and that's the nicest word Aaron could find in his vocabulary to describe the smelly brown stream. He was used to the crystal-clear sparkling waterfall that ran quite literally through his New York treehouse.

Aaron grew up in the elegant foothills of the Hudson Valley. The four-story home was built within and around the forest, with a foundation that crossed the top of a waterfall. Pure elegance and beauty compared to this poverty-stricken city. He wished he could bottle the purity in his world and bring something positive to this region.

The strange realization was that these people seemed happy. Aaron had never met a woman as happy to be alive as Felicia. At least until she learned Aaron and his brothers were planning to stay the night at a fancy hotel in Belize. He would need to drag that story from her. But for now, he would enjoy getting to meet the remainder of her family.

With directions from Felicia and Dominic, the limo driver maneuvered through the narrow streets and up the hills to a rural neighborhood.

Where Felicia's family lived wasn't in the slums, but it was not the kind of place where a limousine would casually pull up and let out three American guys.

Their home was smaller than a farm but had a large garden area with a few chickens and a goat who Aaron remembered was named Lui. The property seemed well-maintained but lived in. With all the kids who came running from inside, Aaron was glad to have a hotel reserved across the river rather than encroach on an already crowded residence.

Not all of the children belonged to Dominic and his wife Yris, but it was nearly impossible to keep track of them, so Aaron didn't try. The adults were all considered aunts and uncles, and the children were all considered cousins.

Felicia seemed to live in the world in between the aunts and the cousins. Not quite an adult, but not one of the children either. Aaron wasn't sure what to think about his relationship with her. She was purity and youthfulness and light wrapped in a colorful, flowing dress that hugged her curves in all the right places, reminding him she was definitely not a child.

Although Aaron was a man—an experienced man—Felicia reached into his heart and made him wish he could turn back time and return to the innocence he saw in her eyes. He felt unworthy of the hero worship that emanated from her and all her little brothers and sisters and cousins. They all wanted to hug Aaron and his brothers. They all wanted to climb inside the limo, which their driver, Joab, graciously allowed.

Aaron was glad Joab had been willing to stay here for the night and suddenly wondered how he would travel around once Joab headed back to Flores. Would he need to rent a car? Take public transportation or a taxi? None of those sounded like something he wanted to do. He wished he could keep a driver but certainly didn't want to travel around in a limousine for days or weeks. Maybe there was a local service. For now, he tried to concentrate on his new friends, or more accurately described, his new family.

After many hours on an airplane and almost two hours in a car, Aaron was thankful to hear that Yris had prepared a big meal. She served a thick and spicy stew called pepián. It boasted a strange combination of pears, squash, carrots, potatoes, and corn, and was served with homemade tortillas and chilled soda in bottles that had not been opened. Aaron was thankful for that. He wasn't prepared for the horror stories relating to drinking water in third world countries. He hoped at least the food would not make him sick but didn't consider the possibilities until halfway through his meal.

Joab was included in the meal and the conversation and treated like one of the family. The adults sat around talking and enjoying the cooling evening, excited to have American cousins visiting. Aaron wished he didn't have to leave, but he and his brothers kept yawning. They promised to return in the morning and tour the city and the area and get to know the family better.

When the time came to head to their hotel, Felicia grew quiet as she walked Aaron to the limo. Hayden and Owen climbed in the car, and Joab waited in the driver's seat while Aaron stood near the back of the car, holding one of Felicia's hands.

"I don't want you to go over to Belize," she finally admitted in Spanish. "They are bad people."

"We're going to stay there tonight, but tomorrow I want you to tell me the story about why you think they are bad people," Aaron said. "Help me understand."

"Okay, I will tell you tomorrow," Felicia said.

"And I want you to show me everything fun about your town and this area and take me to see things that most tourists don't get to see."

"Okay." She chuckled and placed a quick kiss on Aaron's check.

Aaron wished he could pull her into his arms and give her a real kiss but was keenly aware that they had an audience of her mom and dad and aunts and uncles and grandparents. Some other time. He leaned forward and kissed Felicia on her forehead, then waved lightly as he tucked himself into the limo. His brothers chuckled at him when he sighed with a cheesy grin. He was losing his heart to that girl, and they all knew it.

Chapter Three

Belize

"Why do you think Felicia and her father didn't want us to come to Belize?" Aaron asked at breakfast the following morning. "This place is incredible. What's not to like?" He gently speared a chunk of mango with his fork and dipped the fruit into his yogurt parfait.

Since they'd arrived at the San Ignacio Resort, they'd been treated as the royalty they were. But it was more than that. The people seemed genuinely kind and hospitable to all the guests. The rooms were spacious and clean, with more amenities than most typical hotels. The views from their private balcony looked out over the jungle canopy, the rolling foothills, and beyond. And if the dinner menu was as delectable as the breakfast, Aaron wanted to bring Felicia for a date. He just wasn't sure he could drag her across the Mopan River.

"We have had a border dispute for a hundred years or more," Joab explained. "The people in Belize think they should be their own country. Guatemalans feel they should be part of our country." Joab had become a fourth member of their group over the course of twenty-four hours. He was like a local guide, providing valuable information most tourists didn't receive.

"But why do they hate each other?" Aaron asked, setting aside his fork and steepling his hands. "Why did Felicia call the Belizeans 'bad people'?"

"I don't think the Belizeans hate the Guatemalans," Joab said. "I think the Guatemalans hate the Belizeans because someone on the Belizean side of the Adjacency Line has been kidnapping women and children from the El Pilar Mayan reservation."

"Kidnapping?" Hayden's eyes were wide. "Why?"

"Probably as slaves or sex slaves. Or both." Joab shrugged as if that should have been obvious to the brothers. "Human trafficking is a problem worldwide."

"True." Hayden nodded.

"Do you have a different car?" Aaron asked Joab, changing the subject.

"A different... car?" Joab cocked his head to the side and creased his brow.

"Yeah, other than your limousine." Aaron was forming an idea.

"I have a sturdy Toyota Highlander," Joab said. "Good for back roads and hills."

"How would you like a job for the next few weeks?" Aaron asked. "As my driver and tour guide. I can pay for your nightly hotel room here at the resort, and you can drive us back and forth to Felicia's and take us wherever she wants to go. I will continue to pay you double."

"Are you serious?" Joab asked, his bite of cinnamon roll halfway to his mouth.

"Yeah, do you have any family at home? A wife? Children? Something that would keep you from being available over the next few weeks?"

"No, I live with my big family, much like your Felicia does. I am not married."

"I really don't want to take public transportation or hire a taxi every day. And I don't want to rent a car and try to drive myself around. Once my brothers leave, you and I would just be friends hanging out, and a chaperone for me and Felicia so her father doesn't follow us everywhere we go."

"I will need to think about this," Joab said. "And I would need to go home and switch vehicles and pack some clothes."

"Take all the time you need," Aaron said. "I'll reserve your room for tonight in hopes you'll return." He took another bite of his eggs, seeing that the other guys were nearly done with their food.

"That's very generous. Thank you." Joab had been overcome with emotion upon seeing the regal accommodations the night before, but the brothers assured him money was no object.

The guys finished their breakfast and left the restaurant to return to their suites and prepare for the trip back to Felicia's house. They had gone overboard with booking too many rooms and suites so that the brothers could each have their own bedroom within adjoining suites, and Joab was in a separate room down the hall.

Between the three living spaces, they had a total of six beds and sleeping available for fourteen people. No wonder Joab had been overwhelmed. They would need to re-evaluate those arrangements, especially after Hayden and Owen returned to the States.

The drive back down from the beautiful mountainous resort would have been almost depressing, slipping into the reality of city life below, had Aaron not anticipated his reunion with Felicia.

Joab would be dropping them off at her house and heading back to Flores. He hadn't confirmed yet if he was planning to return and take Aaron up on his offer to pay Joab for his continued service as their driver and tour guide. Until they pulled up to the Cohen's home.

Aaron may or may not have texted Felicia to ask if she had a single aunt or cousin to entice Joab to stay. She said her mother's youngest sister was single and would see what she could do.

Sure enough, a young woman sat on the front porch swing beside Felicia. The woman had to be at least twenty-five and a classic Hispanic beauty with dark eyes and skin, and long, brown hair. She rose from the swing, along with Felicia, and together they descended the porch steps.

Joab turned to Aaron and said through the slider window between the front seats of the limo to the back, "If she's single, I'll return in a few hours with my Highlander."

"Thank goodness," Aaron said with a conspiratorial grin and reached over to Hayden and Owen for a fist bump. With one quick text, he had secured himself a driver. He hoped the rest of his vacation in Guatemala would be that easy.

Chapter Four

English as a Second Language

"**B**uenos días," Felicia said with her playful, childlike enthusiasm. She tucked herself into Aaron's arms and kissed him on the cheek. He was tempted to lean down and kiss her lips to return the good morning salutation but reminded himself they were too early in their budding relationship to go that far.

"How are you this morning?" Aaron asked in Spanish. He was getting more comfortable with his new bilingual environment and predicted he'd be fluent in Spanish before he climbed onto a plane to return to the States. He pulled her into a full hug in response to her smile.

"I'm good." Felicia pulled herself back from his arms and nodded toward her aunt. "This is my aunt Kisa. She wanted to come meet you. Kisa is my mother's youngest sister, so she is not related to you."

"Pleasure to meet you," Aaron said, reaching out a hand. "These are my brothers, Hayden and Owen. And *this* is our local guide, Joab. He will be our driver and companion for the duration of our stay." Aaron pulled Joab closer to shake Kisa's hand.

"I hope you'll stay a long time." Kisa's sultry Spanish voice was more mature than Felicia's, and she looked Joab up and down with a subtle message of interest. Aaron reevaluated his original assessment of her age to be closer to thirty. Perfect. Perhaps she'd want to come along on some of their adventures.

"Have you eaten?" Felicia asked. "My mother always has food."

"We ate at the hotel," Aaron told her. "Breakfast was complimentary with our suites."

"What is a suite?" Felicia creased her brow.

"A suite is usually larger than a hotel room and has a living room, plus a bedroom, and sometimes a kitchen," Aaron explained.

"All that space for just the four of you?"

"Well, no." Aaron gulped. "We had three suites between the four of us because two of the suites had more than one bed. And we each wanted our own... bed."

"A whole bed by yourself?" Felicia asked. "That seems like a waste of space."

Aaron was growing uncomfortable with this conversation. "Well, we paid for all the space."

"I can think of more important ways to give away money." She seemed completely serious, as if she were averse to the idea of paying for something unnecessary.

"You're probably right." Aaron cleared his throat.

Owen stepped up beside Aaron and draped an arm over his shoulder. "Maybe we should get a smaller hotel room tonight."

"I'm not sharing a bed with you," Aaron said quietly in English through clenched teeth.

"I'll share a bed with"—Owen answered in a similar fashion and gulped—"Hayden."

"Why do I have to be the one to share a bed?" Hayden asked.

"Did I mention," Felicia's aunt Kisa said in perfect English, "that I attended college at the University of Arizona?"

"You hadn't mentioned that." Aaron gulped and met her gaze. "What was your major?"

"K–12 education with a concentration in English as a second language." Kisa folded her arms and smirked.

"That... is an honorable career choice." Aaron pulled at his collar.

"I agree." Kisa pulled Felicia closer. "That's why I've been teaching my family how to speak English, particularly my young niece here who thinks this hot guy from America is going to marry her someday."

Aaron started coughing, and Hayden laughed so hard he snorted.

"Here, I'll get you a water bottle from the refrigerator," Joab said, ducking into the back of the limo and returning with a cold bottle, which Aaron took gratefully.

Aaron thought quickly about a way to save face on this conversation. He looked right into Felicia's eyes. "Shall we just go ring shopping today, then?"

All of them laughed, and the ice was broken. Dodged that bullet.

"How about a tour of my city instead?" Felicia asked with a grin, switching back to Spanish.

"Sounds wonderful." He followed her lead and resumed her native tongue, assuming she hadn't learned enough English yet to feel comfortable speaking long term.

"Would you like me to drive?" Joab held open the door to his limousine. "I can wait until after lunch to go pick up my Highlander."

"You have a Highlander?" Kisa asked, taking a step closer to Joab. "I've always wanted to go off-roading in one of those."

"I could take you sometime," Joab said breathlessly, as if he'd been smitten by her charm.

"That would be great," Kisa said with a subdued excitement. "Could I sit up front with you? We can let these kids sit in the back."

Joab seemed to forget he was holding the door for his financier and strode to the front of the limo and opened the passenger door for Kisa.

"Why thank you, señor," she said, slipping into the leather seat. "Ooh, fancy."

"Thank you." Joab sighed with a cheesy grin, then shook off his stupor and hurried to the back door. Before Aaron and Felicia entered the car, Joab asked, "Where are we heading?"

"Well, around town would be an easy answer," Felicia answered, continuing in Spanish. "But I promised Aaron I would tell him about my frustration with the people of Belize, so I think we should drive up to El Pilar to see the Mayan reservation."

"We have to drive into Belize to get there." Joab hesitated. "I thought you didn't want to go to Belize."

"This is too important." Felicia lifted her chin, one of the few times her features were firm and resolute.

"Maybe we should wait until after I pick up my Highlander," Joab suggested. "El Pilar is up in the hills and the roads might be impassable with the limo."

"Good point." Felicia sighed. "Okay, around town, then."

They all climbed in, and Joab slowly pulled the limo away from the Cohen's home and wound his way down from the residential neighborhoods into the city.

There was nothing beautiful or impressive about Melchor de Mencos, but Felicia pointed out this and that marketplace, church building, or restaurant.

Aaron held her hand and tried to pay attention. But what he really wanted was to hear more about the Mayan reservation. Maybe after lunch they could take a walk and she could tell him the story without any distractions.

Finally, they made their way back up to her house under the excuse of hunger and the need to use the bathroom.

Felicia's mother, Yris, had food ready for them, and they enjoyed a hearty afternoon meal. Then Joab took off to Flores to pick up his Highlander and promised to be back in time for dinner, upon Yris's insistence.

After Joab was gone and the kitchen was cleaned, Aaron asked Felicia if she would like to introduce him to her pet goat out back.

Thankfully, Owen and Hayden took the hint that they weren't invited because they made excuses about staying inside where there was shade and little cousins to play games with.

Aaron held Felicia's hand all the way back to the pasture where Lui was happily crunching on grasses. She held the goat by the harness so Aaron could pet him. They were in full view of the house, which meant they had plenty of chaperones, but no one could hear their conversation. Aaron petted Lui and asked the question that had been hanging between them for almost twenty-four hours.

"Tell me about El Pilar and Belize."

Chapter Five

Helpless

"El Pilar is a Mayan reservation that sits along the disputed border between Guatemala and Belize." Felicia held her goat by the harness and petted him absentmindedly, averting her gaze from Aaron.

"Which country claims the reservation?" Aaron leaned against the fence that separated the yard from Lui's pasture.

"Neither. They all made an agreement not to fight over the land. Guatemalans can't fight with the Mayans. Belize people can't fight with them, and the Mayans can't fight with either the Belizeans or the Guatemalans."

"What happens if they fight?" Aaron asked.

"If any of them breaks the treaty, there might be a civil war," Felicia said. "But now the people from Belize are kidnapping the daughters and wives of the Mayans, and they are threatening to leave the reservation and fight the Belizean government to get their women back."

"And do you think that's what they should do?"

"Well, someone has to do something." Felicia was either angry or on the verge of tears. "So far nobody's doing anything."

"What about the Belizean government?" Aaron asked.

"The government of Belize has been taken over by a corrupt military leader, Kaiah Amali," Felicia explained. "Kaiah is even having an affair with the prime minister's wife."

"Sounds like an all-around good guy." Aaron made a half-hearted joke. "But getting back to the main topic here. Where are they taking the girls? Joab said something about human trafficking being a problem, and they're kidnapping the girls to use as slaves and sex slaves."

Felicia shuddered and placed her hand over her face. "That just makes me sick." Her voice wavered with unshed tears.

"Hey, come here." Aaron pulled her into his arms and held her. "We'll figure this out. I have friends in some pretty high places, including the United States Senate. Maybe we can get others involved and help solve this problem."

"Thank you," Felicia said into his shirt, her face still pressed up against his chest. "I feel so helpless."

"You're not helpless." Aaron took a half step back and looked her in the eye. "If you hadn't been brave enough to tell me, I would never have known this was happening. Now that I know there's a problem, I can help."

With her looking up at him with those big brown eyes filled with vulnerability, Aaron had a strong desire to lean down and kiss her. He didn't want their first kiss to be standing at the edge of a goat pasture while discussing stolen Mayan girls being sold as sex slaves. Instead, he kissed her forehead and pulled her close to his chest again.

"Take me to El Pilar tomorrow, introduce me to the people, let me see what I can do to help."

"Okay," she said softly. "Thank you, Aaron. I'm so glad you're here."

"Me too." He gave her one last firm hug, then led her toward the house.

Chapter Six

The Road to El Pilar

"Explain this to me as if you were my tour guide," Aaron asked Joab and Kisa, who sat in the front seat of the Highlander. He asked in English because this was too important for his limited vocabulary in Spanish.

"That is what you hired me for, yes?" Joab grinned at Aaron through the rearview mirror. "To be your tour guide." He kept his hands on the steering wheel as they moved away from the Guatemala border and into Belize.

"I actually know the history better than the rest of you," Kisa said.

"Hey, I know the history," Felicia said, in Spanish, her brow creased. She sat in the middle row, her hand permanently attached to Aaron's since the time the guys picked her and Kisa up from their house.

"You're too emotionally involved." Kisa waved her hand dismissively at Felicia, switching back to Spanish in order to chastise her niece. Aaron wondered why Felicia was emotionally involved but didn't want to interrupt Kisa. He needed to understand where they were heading and why. Kisa switched back to English. "The Mayan reservation is mostly within the Adjacency Zone between the borders of Belize and Guatemala."

"You've lost me already," Aaron said. "What's an adjacency zone?"

"Kind of like a buffer zone on either side of the border between the two countries so that people up in that area won't be shot for crossing into the country illegally."

"That's a thing here?" Hayden asked from the third-row seat. He sounded frightened.

"Not that often." Kisa cleared her throat like she was nervous. "Anyway, the situation goes back pretty far in our history because of some treaty made between Spain and Portugal in the late fourteen hundreds, and then a different treaty between Spain and England in the eighteenth century."

"As far as I'm concerned, the only people who really belong there are the Mayans," Felicia said with a huff, grumbling in Spanish. Aaron was beginning to believe that Felicia understood a great deal more than they gave her credit for. She seemed to listen in English but answered in Spanish.

Kisa continued. "Anyway, the Belizean government claims they own the land. The Guatemalan government claims *they* own the land. But like Felicia said, the only people who have ever lived in the area were the Mayans."

"Now the Mayans are forced into this tiny reservation," Felicia said with such passion that Aaron could see what Kisa meant about her being too emotionally involved.

"Do you have family up there or something?" Aaron squeezed her hand gently. "This seems really important to you."

"My best friend growing up is a member of that tribe, and she was forced to go live there." Felicia almost sounded as if she were going to cry. "I haven't seen her since she moved."

"Will you be able to introduce me to her today?" Aaron asked quietly.

"Maybe." There was hope in her eyes.

"Do you talk to her or text or FaceTime or anything?"

"She doesn't have a cell phone."

"What's her name?"

"Xpiayoc," she said.

"Really? Spee-eye-ick?" Aaron tried to recreate the pronunciation of that very strange name.

"Her name means the mythological goddess of matchmaking," Felicia said.

Aaron leaned closer to Felicia and whispered near her ear. "Do you think she'll be able to predict if you and I will ever get married?"

"I don't think we need a goddess to predict that," Felicia whispered back.

Aaron wanted to pull her close and press his lips to hers, but he was aware they had a very captive audience. Instead, he kissed her neck right behind her ear, and she let out a tiny noise that was almost a whimper.

Aunt Kisa cleared her throat from the front seat where she had turned her body to glare at him.

Aaron sat up, forcing his most innocent expression. "What?"

"Hmpf," Kisa said, then warned under her breath. "Watch yourself."

Owen and Hayden both snickered from the back seat.

Aaron didn't let go of Felicia's hand.

"Hey, we're really close to our hotel," Aaron said as they slowed the Highlander through the city of San Ignacio. "We should stop there for dinner on our way home. I'd love to show you ladies our obscenely large hotel suites before we abandon them for something smaller and less ostentatious."

"Yes! I want to see where you sleep!" Felicia was practically bouncing on the seat. That brought more suppressed laughter from the back row and another stern look from Aunt Kisa.

"She didn't mean anything by that," Aaron told Kisa through clenched teeth. "And anyway, I'm a gentleman. I'm not going to take advantage of her youthful innocence."

"I don't trust you, Aaron Sayid," Kisa said, narrowing her eyes.

Aaron gulped. The woman saw right through him. How was he supposed to reconcile the man he had been a year ago with the man he wanted to be? He couldn't go back in time and change his checkered past, but he could temper his own desire for this adorable girl holding his hand. The best he could do was try to stay worthy of her hero worship.

They turned north out of San Ignacio and climbed the foothills toward the reservation. The Highlander took the unpaved mud paths without trouble. The limo would have gotten stuck two minutes up the road. They'd made a good choice waiting.

The dense forest hid secrets from the past, concealing ancient Mayan ruins that were still under threat from looters even though El Pilar had a thriving tourist business and a modern-day tribe of Mayans living just off the beaten path.

That beaten path didn't have access by Highlander, so they needed to hike from the tourist parking lot. Few people knew where the entrance to the reservation began, and the posted signs for private property kept the tourists at bay. But Kisa had been here before and had called ahead to one of the tribal leaders she'd known for years. The tribe knew exactly why the three Americans had hiked down the hills to their home, and the brothers were welcomed with a feast.

Chapter Seven

Where do You Keep Your Slaves?

"Felicia!" A woman came running as Aaron and his brothers entered the plaza with Felicia, Kisa, and Joab.

"Xpiayoc!" Felicia finally released Aaron's hand and ran ahead to give her friend a hug.

Aaron discreetly shook out his hand and wiped the sweat on his jeans. That was the longest time he'd ever held another person's hand. Ten seconds later, he longed to hold her again. He was becoming increasingly addicted to Felicia Cohen.

He approached the reunited childhood friends, staying a few feet back until Felicia realized he was there and pulled him close to introduce him to Xpiayoc. The woman pulled him into a hug and said something in a language he didn't understand.

"She's welcoming you to her village," Felicia translated into Spanish. "They all understand the ancient Mayan language even though they mostly speak Spanish."

"Do you know how to speak the Mayan language?" Aaron asked Felicia, realizing a little more how smart she was. Her childlike jubilance hid her intelligence well, and he wondered if she used that to her advantage.

"Just a few phrases," Felicia said. "That one's easy because it's so commonly used."

"Thank you for that warm welcome," Aaron said in Spanish, turning to Felicia's friend. "Do you understand me?"

"Of course, I understand you," Xpiayoc answered in Spanish. "Although, you are not very good at speaking Spanish."

"No, I'm not," Aaron acknowledged. "But I'm learning as quickly as I can. I have the best teacher in the world." He pulled Felicia close and wrapped his arm around her back.

"And I am learning a little bit of English," Felicia said in Spanish, pride creeping into her voice.

"Is this your husband?" Xpiayoc asked Felicia.

Aaron realized he hadn't introduced himself. "I am Aaron Sayid, Felicia's future husband."

"Oh really?" Felicia looked up at him with a playful grin. "You have finally resigned yourself to the inevitability?"

"Honey, I resigned myself the first time I looked into your eyes." They locked gazes for a few seconds, and something passed between them that was powerful. Then they were interrupted.

"Let me get you some food, and we can explain the situation with our missing daughters," Xpiayoc said, waving them along.

He and Felicia followed, once again holding hands. Aaron felt whole again just connecting with her. He was keenly aware of his brothers behind him along with Kisa and Joab.

The food was delicious and abundant. A spicy meat with rice and homemade tortillas. Aaron's mouth watered when the plate was placed before him.

He lost his appetite once the tribal chief began speaking.

"There is a stream nearby that we use to bathe and wash clothing. The first time one of our girls went missing, we believe she went down to take a bath. She never came back. We insisted no one travel outside the immediate village alone. The second time, two girls disappeared at once."

Aaron looked around the area they referred to as the village and couldn't find any clearly defined boundaries. The trees were dense, the ground uneven and rocky, houses were built haphazardly and without design. The ancient structures of the Mayans were covered in hundreds of years of vegetation until the beauty that likely reigned in this area was shrouded and unrecognizable.

"Do you know for certain the girls were taken by people rather than wild animals?" Aaron asked.

"Yes, one of the younger girls in our tribe saw the two teenage girls being stolen by two men. The little girl couldn't even scream fast enough to get anyone's attention. She ran back to get help but, by then, there was no trace of the girls or the men. They had disappeared."

"Did the little girl give a good description of the men?" Aaron asked.

"She said the men's skin was light, very light compared to the girls."

"That doesn't sound like Belizeans," Owen said. "Sounds more like Americans or Europeans."

"Americans are the people paying big dollars to purchase sex slaves." Joab's statement was so matter of fact he could have been talking about the weather. "Dark skinned beauties are in high demand. Especially virgins."

"That's terrible." Felicia tucked herself into Aaron's side as if afraid she'd be the next person kidnapped if Aaron didn't protect her.

He wrapped his arm around her and pulled her close, hoping to reassure her that he'd never let anything happen to her. He wished he could make sure nothing happened to any other girls.

"How many girls have gone missing," Kisa asked.

"Twenty-four," the tribal leader said. There was a collective gasp between Aaron, his brothers, Felicia, and Kisa. Joab didn't seem surprised. Or if he was, he didn't let his face show his emotions. "We are at a loss what to do."

"Let us give it some thought and consult with our families," Aaron said. "Our grandfather is a United States senator. He might have some ideas as well, especially if we can somehow prove that Americans are involved."

"If we don't know where they've gone or who took them, how can you prove there are Americans involved?" Xpiayoc asked.

"I suspect we do know where they've been taken," Joab said. "There is a thriving sex-trade and human trafficking operation in the harbor town of Belize City."

"Good, we can go find our missing girls," Felicia said with excitement.

"It's not so easy." Joab shook his head with sympathy. "You can't just go walking up to the men and ask where they're keeping their slaves. Especially a pretty girl like you."

Felicia tucked herself close to Aaron again.

"Why isn't someone doing something about this?" Aaron was beyond frustrated and having trouble keeping his anger at bay.

"There is a great deal of corruption within the Belizean government," Joab said. "One of the many reasons why Felicia didn't want you to come to Belize. You are patronizing the enemy."

"You sure know a great deal about all of this for just being a limo driver," Aaron said with suspicion.

"Yes, I do." Joab grinned with pride. "You'd be surprised what people say in the back of your limo when they don't think you're listening and assume you don't understand English."

"Huh... good point." Aaron thought back to some of the things he and his brothers had done in the back seats of limousines. He glanced at Hayden and Owen, and all three of them cringed. "Well, this has been an enlightening conversation."

"How about if we take you for a tour of the village, and you can get a better idea of where the girls were taken from and possibly interview the families involved," the tribal leader said.

Aaron wanted to remind the man that they were not detectives but decided to follow the man's direction. Maybe later, he and his brothers could brainstorm with Felicia, Kisa, and Joab. He was determined to help somehow.

Chapter Eight

A Bed to Yourself

"Oh my gosh! You have this whole bed to yourself?" Felicia climbed up onto the king-sized bed in Aaron's hotel suite. Aaron had made good on his promise to take the girls to dinner at the resort and show them their ostentatious hotel rooms. Felicia was particularly drawn to Aaron's bed. "I want to sleep on this bed." She sprawled her arms and legs as far as she could reach in all directions.

Aaron's jaw dropped, and he groaned in frustration, bumping his head against the side of the doorjamb. "You've got to be kidding me."

"Good luck with that, dude." Owen patted Aaron on the shoulder as he brushed passed to enter his own hotel room.

Hayden paused and draped his arm around Aaron in mock solidarity. His voice was low and sympathetic. "How long's it been, man?"

"Too long," Aaron squeaked out. "Help."

"This is all you," Hayden said. "I'll echo Owen's sentiment. Good luck." Hayden did the unthinkable. He walked away. Leaving Aaron alone with the most beautiful girl he'd ever met lying across his bed.

"You should come sit with me," Felicia said, maneuvering up to lay her head on one of the pillows. "This is the greatest bed I've ever seen." If she knew how tempting she was, she wouldn't be encouraging him. Then again, maybe she would.

"I respect her. I respect me. I respect her father," Aaron chanted softly as he thumped his forehead against the doorframe again. "Her father would kill me. My father would kill me. My mother would kill me. Her mother would probably feed me. Okay, that decides it."

Aaron pushed away from the doorframe, leaving the door wide open just in case his body didn't realize he was joking. With controlled strides, he walked across the room, reminding himself with each step that nothing was going to happen.

He would keep his hands to himself. He would keep his thoughts as pure as he possibly could. He would calm himself so he could concentrate on getting to know Felicia as the beautiful human being she was and not the beautiful body that was lying on his bed.

Sitting cautiously on the edge of the bed, he swung one leg up and then the other, maintaining distance by facing her rather than sitting beside her. She wasn't having that. Felicia sat up and reached for him, tickling him beneath his arms. That set him off, and he had to retaliate, tackling her in the process.

Felicia squealed playfully as Aaron tickled her and nuzzled his face against her neck, placing a quick kiss there before she could object. Not that she would have. He could easily take complete advantage of her, and she would have been willing to get carried away.

He reigned in his own desires and stopped tickling her, instead he lay beside her and propped himself up on one elbow, gazing down into her now serene face.

"You like my bed, huh?" Aaron asked, lifting a strand of hair off her face.

"I've never slept in a bed this big," she said. "Heck, I don't usually get to sleep in a bed by myself."

"If you slept in *this* bed, you wouldn't be by yourself." Aaron was aware that his voice lowered, and his breathing increased.

"Yes, I'm aware of that," she answered, her lids heavy and more sensual than they'd been the moment before.

"Are you?" Aaron pulled his bottom lip between his teeth, knowing from experience what his sultry gaze did to women. "And is that something you want?"

"I want"—she paused for dramatic effect—"a lot of things."

"Most of which you are not going to get right this moment." Aaron lifted his hand and tapped his finger on the end of her nose. "Because I respect you."

She sighed playfully. "Darn."

"My sentiment exactly." Aaron scrutinized her as if from afar and twisted his face in mock consideration. "There is one thing I can give you right now."

"What is it?" Felicia's hand wrapped into the fabric of Aaron's shirt, and she pulled him a little closer.

"Your first kiss," he whispered.

"How do you know it would be my first kiss?" she asked.

"Will it be?" he baited her.

"Yeah..."

"Good guess, then."

"What about you?" she asked. "Have you ever kissed a girl before?"

"What do you think?" Aaron averted his eyes.

"I think you've probably kissed many, many girls."

"Does that bother you?" Still avoiding her gaze, he toyed with the hem of her shirt where it rested just over the side pocket of her jeans.

"Have you kissed any girls since you met me?"

"Since you called me last week?" Aaron returned his gaze to hers. "No, I have not kissed any girls since you called me."

"Do you want to kiss any girls besides me?" she asked.

"No, ma'am, I do not."

"Then what does it matter how many girls you've kissed in the past?"

"What if I've done a lot more than just *kiss* girls?" He wondered if this was the moment she would push him away and run from the room crying, discovering that the man of her dreams had defiled himself. Repeatedly. Who had not waited a day beyond puberty to begin experimenting with any girl he could get his hands on. Who had done things he'd be embarrassed to talk about, even with his brothers or his best friends.

"I'll repeat my previous question," she said in all seriousness. "Do you want to be with any girls besides me?"

Aaron shook his head softly, not daring to speak, not daring to believe that she would offer forgiveness that readily.

"Then what does it matter how many girls are in your past?" she whispered. "Everything from your past made you into the man you are today. The man I'm sort of crazy about."

"The man you're crazy about is sort of crazy about you too," Aaron said.

"I know." Felicia gripped her hand into his shirt again, pulling him down to meet her lips.

Drawing from years of experience, having learned what women want from a man, Aaron took his time, softly, gently, a feather touch before molding his lips to hers, deepening a kiss that could arguably be the best first kiss a girl could ever want.

"Oh, heck no! Get your hands off my niece," Kisa said from the doorway.

Aaron was glad he'd left the door open and simultaneously frustrated that he'd left the door open. He groaned and pulled away slightly, his eyes unapologetically locked with Felicia's. "Don't worry, Aunt Kisa," he said. "I wouldn't have done anything."

"Yeah right." Kisa huffed and turned to leave the room. "Come on. Let's go to dinner."

"She wants to go to dinner," Aaron whispered down to Felicia, who still lay in the crook of his arm, still gazing up at him with bedroom eyes.

"She must be as hungry as I am," Felicia answered, also in a whisper.

"I doubt either of you are even close to being as hungry as I am." Aaron leaned forward and placed another sweet kiss on Felicia's lips, then reluctantly pulled away and extricated himself from her arms. "Come on. Let's go to dinner."

Chapter Nine

Cordially Invited

Aaron and his brothers received a group text simultaneously and pulled their cell phones from their pockets. A family group text was often life-changing news, like someone has died and we're flying to Saudi Arabia. Get packed. This one was just as shocking.

They stopped the game they were playing with all the little cousins in the street outside of Felicia's house. The brothers were losing anyway. The cousins thought it was funny that they could beat Aaron and his brothers at Chasumcas because they knew the rules better, or maybe they kept changing the rules. The brothers had a tendency to play the game as if it were soccer, which it wasn't. They weren't really playing to win, just to keep the little cousins busy while the ladies prepared an evening meal.

Aaron, Hayden and Owen walked toward one another with their phones in hand, and when they were far enough away from the kids, Aaron read out loud, "You are cordially invited to attend the wedding of your brother, Prince Augustus Sayid to the lovely Phoebe Harris on Saturday, the twenty-sixth of June, at three in the afternoon. Please prepare to return from your vacation." The text was from Alex Stephenson, Junior, Gus's best f riend.

"You've got to be kidding me." Owen's jaw dropped.

"I'm declaring the wager right now," Hayden said. "Pregnant? Or not pregnant?"

"Pregnant," Owen said confidently.

"Not pregnant," Aaron said. "Gus wouldn't do that."

Owen and Hayden both snickered.

"Have you seen the way they look at each other?" Owen asked. "This was inevitable."

"I thought he had turned his life around." Aaron's heart sunk.

"A man only has so much willpower," Hayden said. "Believe me, I know."

"You had better not get the king's daughter pregnant," Aaron warned.

"The Princess Miranda is in New York City, attending college under the watchful eye of her older brother, Prince Ethan. I don't think there's any danger of that."

"You'd be surprised how easy it is to make the wrong choice under the right circumstances." Aaron glanced across the yard as the beautiful Felicia Cohen set a stack of paper plates on the picnic table. She looked up and smiled back at him. "Too easy."

"Well, it looks as if we'll be packing up and heading home to America," Owen said.

Hayden wrapped his arm around his brother's shoulders and followed Aaron's gaze. "Whatcha gonna do about *that*?"

"Find out if she has a passport." With his phone still in his hand and the text message on the screen, Aaron strode, with purpose, across the yard to where Felicia was helping her mother and aunt lay out food for dinner.

"Ladies, can I steal Felicia for a moment?" Aaron didn't wait for them to answer. He just snaked his arm around Felicia's back and pulled her gently away. When he had her sufficiently out of earshot, he whispered, "I need to speak with you and your father."

"My father?" Felicia's purposely innocent expression and batting eyelashes told Aaron she knew exactly what he wanted to ask her father. "He's probably in his office."

Perfect. Dominic would be ready to talk business if there was a desk between them. The first part of this conversation needed to stay professional. Aaron took Felicia's hand and led her into the house to the office where her father ran their business and household finances.

"Padre?" Felicia knocked on her father's open door, and Dominic lifted his head, pulling his attention away from the ledger on his desk. "Can we interrupt you for a moment?"

"Of course." Dominic removed his reading glasses and tucked them into the collar of his shirt. "What can I do for you?"

"Sir, I just received a text asking us to return to the States because our youngest brother is getting married in a few days."

"You're leaving?" Felicia gripped Aaron's hand tighter.

"Well, that's the thing, I wondered if... maybe"—Aaron glanced at Felicia and then squared his shoulders and faced her father—"if maybe Felicia could come home with me to the States. There will be a lot of extended family at the wedding, and she could meet her cousins."

"Oh! Please, Daddy, can I go?" Felicia sounded so young begging her father's permission to leave the country even though she was twenty-one years old.

Aaron felt just as old fashioned asking her father's permission, but these were the traditions he needed to respect.

"He's very young." Dominic's brow creased. "Are you talking about Augustus?"

"Yes, Gus and Phoebe, his high school girlfriend." Aaron let his statement hang in the air, waiting to see what Dominic would say.

"Do you plan to return to Guatemala?" Dominic asked.

Aaron wasn't sure if Dominic was asking Aaron or Felicia. He decided just to answer in the collective. "We still need to help rescue the Mayan girls who have been stolen from their families. So, yes, we'll be back."

"True..." Dominic tapped his pencil against his lips.

"We'll also have the opportunity to talk to my grandfather, Senator Alejandro Cohen," Aaron said. "He might have some suggestions on how to get help from the U.S. government."

"Your grandfather is my uncle." Dominic raised his eyebrows. "I'd forgotten about that."

"Maybe you'd like to come with us also?" Aaron suggested.

"I have a business to run here. But thank you for the offer."

"Can I go, Padre?" Felicia asked.

"You don't have a passport." Dominic sounded as if he was looking for a reason to forbid her to go but didn't really have one. After all, his daughter was an adult.

"There's time. I can get one."

"Well, let's see if that's possible before I make any promises."

"Oh, thank you, Papa!"

This was almost an admission of acceptance. But there was one more thing that Aaron needed to do. He turned to Felicia.

"Could I have a moment alone with your father?"

"Of course," she said, rising from her chair. "I'll just go help with dinner." She leaned down and kissed Aaron on the cheek. He wanted more than a kiss on the cheek, but he would have to wait until later for that.

As Felicia left the room, Aaron pulled the door shut so that he had Dominic's attention all to himself and privacy for this part of the conversation.

"Sir, I think you know why I want to speak with you, so I won't beat around the bush. I'm not going to presume that Felicia will be willing, but I would like your blessing to request her hand in marriage, if, while we are visiting America, I get the impression that she would like to be my wife. I don't want to take away her right to choose by asking you exclusively for your permission, but I would like your blessing to ask her if she wants to marry me."

"I have no doubt in my mind what Felicia's answer will be," Dominic said with a chuckle.

"Nor do I," Aaron said with a relieved, shaky breath. "But what are your thoughts on the subject?"

"I can't think of a better man to take care of my little girl."

"Thank you, sir." Aaron lowered his gaze and wrung his hands in his lap. "I haven't always been the kind of man worthy of your daughter. But I will do the best I can to make myself worthy going forward."

"I know you will, son," Dominic said. "We all have a past, and not one of us is perfect."

"Thank you for your grace." Aaron felt as if a weight had been lifted from his shoulders now that he'd admitted to Felicia and her father that he had made some bad choices as a youth.

"Now, go do some research and find out what it's going to take to get that girl a passport," Dominic said. "It's time you introduce her to *your* family and ask for their blessing as well."

"Right away, sir." Aaron hopped up from his chair and reached for Dominic's hand in a show of respect. He thanked the man he was certain to be his future father-in-law and hurried from the room.

Chapter Ten

Let's Go Shopping

"Let me see if we're all on the same page," Aaron said, glancing around the table at his brothers and friends. "The six of us pile into Joab's Highlander—"

"If we all fit with luggage and everything," Hayden interrupted.

"—if we all fit," Aaron acknowledged. "Then we'll drive to Flores and drop Hayden and Owen off at the airport so they can return to the States."

"Oh, yeah, I'm looking forward to some good Middle Eastern cuisine." Owen rubbed his belly in anticipation.

"Maybe we should stop at the Garden House down in Rosendale on our way home," Hayden suggested. He and Owen reached out for a fist bump.

"You guys can do whatever the heck you want once you return to the States, but let's get back on track." Aaron was excited to get this planned. "The rest of us will drive south to Guatemala City, find the passport issue center or embassy or whatever they call it, get Felicia fingerprinted, photographed, and issued a passport—"

"Which is going to cost a small fortune," Felicia said in a hesitant voice.

Aaron considered her hesitancy. He knew she was excited to come with him to the States. But that was about the fifth time she'd been concerned about money since he'd met her. He'd have to look deeper into that one of these days. For now, he needed to get her onto an airplane and take her home with him.

"I have plenty of money, darling. It's okay." Aaron lifted their adjoined hands and kissed the back of hers, then continued, bringing a little humor into the conversation. "You and I will board a jet in Guatemala City and Joab and Kisa can ride off into the sunset together and live happily ever after."

"Until you return to the Republic and require my services again to drive you around so you can solve all the problems in Central America and bring about world peace," Joab said.

Everyone chuckled at Joab's joke, not acknowledging Aaron's insinuation that Joab and Kisa were officially a couple.

"Exactly," Aaron said. "Everyone on board?"

They all nodded.

"Let's get packing." Owen stood and pushed his chair back.

"Uh... I don't own a suitcase," Felicia said.

"Guess it's time to go shopping." Aaron stood and offered her his hand.

"I don't have a lot of money." Felicia spoke softly, turning her head as if speaking to just Aaron even though there were four other people in the room.

"Let's you and I go take a walk out to the pasture and check on Lui," Aaron whispered. He took her hand and pulled her gently away from the table. This had been a stroll they'd taken several times in the past few days since Aaron arrived in Guatemala. The goat pasture was within view of the house, but away from listening ears.

"Okay." Felicia allowed Aaron to lead her out the back door.

"Do you remember when we first spoke on the phone?" Aaron asked when they were far enough from the house. "You told me you could never afford to come to the States. Remember?"

"Yes, I remember." They had reached the fence where Lui hurried over to have his nose rubbed.

"And what did I do?" Aaron asked.

"You came here instead."

"Now that I'm here, I want to bring you back with me." Aaron reached out a finger and lifted Felicia's chin so that she met his gaze. "I invited you to come with me, and I intend to pay for everything we do, everywhere we go, everything we eat. I want to spoil you like the princess that you are."

"I'm not a princess, Aaron."

"When you're on the arm of a prince... you're a princess."

"Are you my prince charming?" Felicia had a tiny smile playing along her lips.

"If you'll have me as your prince charming." Aaron's heart raced with happiness and love and devotion wrapped up in the mysteriously colorful eyes of this Hispanic beauty standing before him. "For now, let me buy you a suitcase, and an airplane ticket, and take you home with me so you can meet my parents, and see if you like the United States as much as you think you will. Heck, you might hate it there and decide I'm not such a charming prince after all."

"I doubt that." Felicia playfully slapped Aaron on his chest, and he took the advantage to pull her into his arms.

"There's something I've wanted to do for hours." Aaron's voice lowered to a husky whisper.

"What have you wanted to do?" Felicia lifted her face to his as if she already suspected.

"I want to kiss you again," he whispered.

"Do you think anyone's watching from the house?" she whispered back.

"I really don't care." Aaron closed the distance between them and molded his lips to hers, pulling her body close until every nerve ending in his body connected with every nerve ending in hers. He wanted to kiss her every day and night for the rest of his life, but one hurdle at a time.

Lui pushed his furry nose between them, demanding attention from the girl who fed him every day. Aaron and Felicia both chuckled as they were separated.

"Someday, I'm going to have the chance to kiss you and no one will interrupt us," Aaron said.

"Someday," she whispered back.

"For now, let's go shopping." He raised his eyebrows, waiting for her to agree.

"Okay," she finally said. "Let's go shopping."

Chapter Eleven

Introductions

"Look at you, stud," Aaron said as he walked into the tux shop where his youngest brother Gus was getting fitted for his tux. "You're all grown up."

"Aaron!" Gus turned to his oldest brother, causing the tailor to poke himself with a straight pin. He swore under his breath, but that didn't stop Gus from hopping off the low podium and rushing over to hug his brother.

Owen and Hayden also came over to hug Aaron, then their father, and finally Alex, Jr., all of whom were already dressed in their tuxes. Seemed Aaron was the last guy to be fitted.

Aaron's plane had been delayed by a thunderstorm over Guatemala City, typical for summer in Central America. He was cutting things close, arriving two days before Gus's wedding anyway. Having come straight from the airport to the tux shop, Aaron brought a guest.

He glanced carefully around the dressing room before asking, "Is everyone fully dressed in here?"

Not waiting for a firm answer, Aaron ducked back out the curtained dressing area and re-entered holding Felicia's hand. Walking into a room full of mostly strangers, Felicia clung to Aaron's arm with an unusual and temporary shyness.

"Felicia!" Owen stepped forward and pulled her into a hug, as did Hayden. That helped break down her shell.

With a big smile, she hugged them back, already relaxing into her bubbly personality.

Most of the guys knew enough Spanish to hold a full conversation, but Aaron didn't worry about their ability to understand her. He focused his attention on Felicia, introducing them in her native language.

"This is my father, Prince Marcos Sayid," Aaron said in Spanish, gently leading her forward.

"A pleasure to finally meet you," his dad answered, also in Spanish, as he pulled her into a hug.

"You as well," Felicia said, allowing herself to be engulfed in his father's warm embrace.

"And this is my youngest brother, Gus," Aaron said, guiding her away from his father. "He's the one who's getting married."

"Congratulations," Felicia said, also hugging Gus.

"And over here is my brother's best friend, Alex."

Alex and Felicia shook hands rather than her trying to awkwardly lean over his wheelchair.

"Alex is also your third cousin," Aaron told Felicia. "His father, Alexander, was the only son of Alexandria, who was your grandfather's sister."

"So many cousins." Felicia laughed with a shake of her head. "How will I remember everyone?"

"You don't have to remember anyone." Aaron wrapped his arm around her and rubbed her shoulder. "We have a big family."

"We also have a big day ahead of us," his father said. "So, let's get you fitted for your tux. You two are probably exhausted from your flight and want to get home. Can I help you find a couple of bottles of water and some snacks?" He guided Felicia over to a settee near an elegant refrigerated cooler stocked full of drinks and finger foods.

Aaron left his girlfriend in good hands and followed the tailor into a nearby private dressing room. He stepped into his tux and entered the main dressing area, then stood on the low platform for his fitting.

He watched the guys fussing over Felicia and knew she would blend in just fine with his family. This confirmed what he already had decided. He planned to marry that girl, and soon.

Chapter Twelve

A Birth Certificate and a Passport

"What do you think of my parents' house?" Aaron asked Felicia. He leaned against the doorframe of the nicest guest bedroom of the tree house. Aaron had insisted his new girlfriend should have the largest room with the most luxurious bathroom suite, the best view of the waterfall, and most importantly, the largest bed. He wanted her to be pampered beyond her limited imagination.

"This is incredible. I've never seen anything like it." Most people had never seen anything like the tree house that had been literally built over a waterfall on the Landsman River in New York's beautiful Hudson Valley.

"How do you like America?"

"I love it. I never thought I would ever have a chance to come here." Felicia pulled her legs up and wrapped her arms around her knees like an excited little girl stuck within the incredible body of the woman he'd fallen in love with. The king-sized bed where she was surrounded by pillows and comforters was larger than her entire bedroom back home. The bedroom she shared with two of her sisters.

"Any chance you might like to make America a more permanent location to live?" Why was he nervous all of a sudden? Felicia had been the one who had instigated their meeting. She had called Aaron all the way from her father's small, crowded home in Guatemala, practically insisting that they were meant to be together. She had followed him to America to attend his brother's wedding and hadn't stopped smiling since the private jet landed.

"I would love that." Felicia's voice softened as if she could tell the conversation had shifted from the excitement of visiting his family's home to an invitation for them to take their relationship to the next level. "Any chance you would be interested in having me here on a more permanent basis?"

"I think I would love to have you here. But I think I would want you to be my wife first."

She gulped but didn't answer him, the expression on her face both expectant and stunned.

"I'm having a really hard time with you here in that bed and not being able to climb in next to you." Aaron's voice lowered to a frustrated huskiness.

"I'm having a really hard time not inviting you to climb in next to me."

"I don't like the idea of taking you back to your parents' house and dropping you off and then going to my hotel room and not seeing you again for a whole night."

"Then don't." Her eyes beckoned him to take her with him to his hotel room.

"You would need to be my wife in order to spend the night with me."

"Then make me your wife."

"How would your parents feel if you came home to Guatemala as a married woman?" he asked.

"They would probably throw a feast in celebration."

"They wouldn't be angry with you?" Aaron hesitated. "Or angry with me?"

"They would be angrier if you defiled me before we were married," Felicia said. "And the way I feel right now, all I want is for you to come here and lay with me."

"Did you bring your birth certificate and passport with you?"

"Of course, I would not have been able to come into America without it."

"Would you like to come with me tomorrow down to the courthouse and apply for a marriage license?" Aaron asked.

"I would very much like that."

Aaron could barely breathe. "I want to marry you, Felicia."

"I want to marry you too, Aaron."

"I should probably do this correctly." Aaron walked forward toward the bed, lowered himself to his knees and took her hands in his. "Felicia Cohen, will you do me the honor becoming my bride?"

"Yes, Prince Aaron Sayid, I will."

Aaron didn't hesitate. He climbed onto the bed with her and held her in his arms and pressed his lips to hers.

He kissed her for almost an hour, wishing he could do more, looking forward to the next few days when he would be allowed to do more. When he would be allowed to show her physically everything he had wanted to tell her emotionally.

Aaron wanted to finally make love to a woman he loved instead of having a one-night stand, or worse. He now knew that sex was not meant to be casual; it was meant to be shared between two people who loved one another and were joined in legal matrimony. He never dreamed he would think this. A lot had happened in the past year, and Aaron was a changed man.

Felicia was the woman Aaron wanted to be with for the rest of his life, and he wanted to start his life right now. But he loved and respected her enough, and he respected himself enough, to wait another day or two.

Aaron dragged all the willpower he had inside himself in order to leave Felicia's bed and walk down the hall and climb into his own.

Chapter Thirteen

Inestimable

"Your Highness, may I have a word with you?" Aaron paused at the entryway to his parents' bedroom early Friday morning. He seemed to stand in entryways frequently of late.

"Son? What can we do for you?" His father, Prince Marcos Sayid, once again serving as crown prince to his cousin, the recently crowned king of Madain Saleh, sat at his rolltop desk in the corner of the bedroom suite he shared with the most beautiful princess in the world, Aaron's mother, Hazel Cohen-Sayid.

His mother stepped out of her adjoining bathroom, with a cosmetic compact in one hand and a makeup brush in the other. Her eyes amused, she grinned and predicted correctly, "Let me guess, you've come to raid my jewelry closet."

There wasn't even a question in her prediction, merely an acknowledgement. She stepped back into the bathroom and set her cosmetics on the counter, then entered their large walk-in closet and began turning the dial on the safe.

"After that two-hour make-out session last night, this was inevitable," she said.

"That was less than an hour and the door was open the whole time," Aaron justified.

"Yes, I know, son. I've been around this block a few times. At least you didn't get your girlfriend pregnant as your brother did." She glanced up with apprehension. "Or did you?"

"Wait, what? Who's pregnant?" Aaron felt like he'd been punched in the chest.

"Oh, oops, didn't realize he hadn't told you. Kinda thought you kids were closer than that."

"I have been out of the country for three weeks," Aaron said, his head swimming. "No one tells me anything. Is the Princess Miranda pregnant? Or Phoebe? Or... did Owen somehow get a girlfriend I don't know about?"

"Seriously? You have to ask?" His mom raised her eyebrows. "Who's getting married tomorrow?"

"Gus and Phoebe..." Aaron whispered.

"Why else would someone get married a month after high school when they were barely eighteen?"

"Uh... princess?" his dad interrupted. "You and I were married less than two months after your high school graduation, and you had just turned eighteen."

"Eh, you just married me so you could force a crown on my head and give me a title." She waved her hand dismissively.

"Don't forget a gleaming white palace and free rein with a paintbrush," his dad reminded her.

"You guys aren't making any sense. I'm extremely disappointed in my youngest brother, and can I please raid your jewelry closet? I'd like to take Felicia over to the courthouse this afternoon so tonight we will be legally allowed to close the door to the guest bedroom and hope that the rush of water from the waterfall drowns out any sounds that may escape that room."

"That was way more information than your mother wanted to hear," she said. "But I'm glad you're doing things in the correct order for the first time since you realized you were a man, and that girls existed. Take your pick." She stepped back and held open the door to her safe.

"Thank you, Mother, for that grim reminder of my not-so-distant sinful past." Aaron stepped into the closet, kissed his mother's cheek, and leaned closer to the gleaming selection. "Got any suggestions?"

"Well, girls love diamonds, but Felicia originates from a humble neighborhood so she's not going to want something too ostentatious..." She perused the selection, then picked out a simple but elegant diamond ring that could have been a hundred year's old. "This belonged to your great-grandmother, Princess Lyla Sayid, and is one of only a few surviving Le Vian diamond rings crafted in Persia in the late seventeen hundreds. She found this at a jewelry bazaar and paid next to nothing for it—a few thousand dollars, I think—took it home to New York City the next time she visited her parents, and the jeweler said the value is inestimable."

"Mom, I can't take that!" Aaron stepped back and lifted his hands in the air in case his mother tried to force the priceless piece of jewelry into his hand. "What if it got lost?"

"What if it got left in a safe for hundreds of years more and no one ever relished its beauty?" she asked, holding the little ring out for Aaron's inspection. "Someone should enjoy this ring. Your bride deserves to be treated like a princess even though we won't be holding a coronation at the courthouse and even though she'll probably never understand its value. She's marrying a prince, for heaven's sake. Let her wear the jewelry of a princess."

With tears pricking the corners of his eyes, Aaron carefully lifted the priceless diamond ring from his mother's hand. "Are you sure about this?"

"Positive." His mom's whisper was husky with emotion. "Now go marry that woman before you do something as stupid as your brother did. *Attempt* to make it to the chapel in time for the rehearsal dinner tonight."

"If I'm getting married this afternoon, I make no promises that I'll be presentable in mixed company for the rehearsal dinner tonight."

"Son, I expect to see you there and on time," his dad said, never having risen from his chair at his desk where he was typing something on his laptop.

"Yes, Your Highness," Aaron said with apologetic remorse.

"And, come here, son." Prince Marcos rose from his seat as Aaron crossed the room, and his dad pulled him into his arms. "I'm proud of you. I don't think I tell you that often enough."

"Love you, Dad," Aaron whispered.

"Love you too, my boy," his dad said. They pulled away and looked each other in the eye, man-to-man. "Oh, and don't forget to bring a couple of your brothers with you to the courthouse. You'll need two witnesses."

"Hadn't thought of that. Thanks for the reminder." Aaron crossed the room and gave his mom one more hug. "I'm going to get married."

Aaron hurried from his parents' bedroom suite, more excited than he could remember ever being in his life. He was getting married.

Chapter Fourteen

Dalton

"How on earth are we supposed to stay dressed long enough to sit through tonight's rehearsal dinner?" Aaron mumbled close to Felicia's ear, pulling her hair aside to trail kisses along her throat.

"They don't actually need us there, right?" Felicia reached for the buttons of Aaron's shirt. "Let's just stay here."

"Your Highness, need I remind you that you are in mixed company?" the limo driver called from the front seat. "You may want to wait until later tonight for any further... uh... entanglements."

Aaron groaned and reluctantly shifted Felicia so that she was no longer straddling his waist, and set her on his legs sideways. A much less compromising position. She snuggled into his arms as if he were holding a baby. He could still feel every inch of her body where a regrettably present article of clothing draped between him and his new bride. He admitted the limo driver had a point. He needed to calm down and wait for later tonight. As tortuous as that would be.

"My father warned me that we needed to be there, and be on time," Aaron told Felicia, not expecting the limo driver, Dalton, to answer.

"Which is why I'm breaking the speed limit on your behalf because I had to drag you out of bed by your ears," Dalton said.

"I could fire you for that," Aaron said.

"No, you can't. Your father has been paying my salary longer than you've been alive. And I'd bet a million dollars he'd take my side over yours on this one."

"You don't have a million dollars," Aaron said.

"How do you know? Your father pays me handsomely to be at his beck and call. And unfortunately, *your* beck and call," Dalton grumbled.

"I usually drive myself," Aaron said. "It's not my fault he made you come back for me."

"He knew you wouldn't get out of bed on time and you'd ruin your brother's rehearsal dinner. There are going to be senators, royalty, and dignitaries at this wedding, you know."

"Yes, I'm very aware of that," Aaron said. "Present company included."

"Are you mad at each other?" Felicia asked with true concern on her face.

"Yes," Aaron said.

"No," Dalton said simultaneously. "Your husband is very easy to tease. He always has been."

"He calls it teasing," Aaron said. "I call it torture and abuse."

"You don't know the definition of torture and abuse," Dalton said.

"Actually, I do." That sobered Aaron right up and calmed his body down. Thinking of all those girls who were still in captivity made him feel guilty that he and Felicia were in America instead of trying to rescue them. He gently moved his bride off his lap and held her hand. "That's why we need to make it a point to have a conversation with Senator Alejandro Cohen at the reception. We need to see if we can get some help from the U.S. government."

"Do you think he will help us?" Felicia asked, biting her lower lip. That was very distracting, but Aaron attempted to focus his thoughts.

"I hope so," Aaron said. "He is my grandfather, after all."

"Is there anything the senator can actually do to help though?" Dalton asked.

"I don't know," Aaron answered honestly. Aaron's first thought was how forward the limo driver was being to butt into their private conversation, but then Aaron remembered that Dalton knew way more than Aaron did about pretty much everything. By sitting in Dalton's limo, Aaron had de facto included Dalton in their conversation. Plus, he and Felicia needed all the help they could get.

Chapter Fifteen

The More things Change

Phoebe didn't look pregnant. Of course, what did Aaron know about anyone looking pregnant?

She looked happy.

Gus looked happy.

The rehearsal dinner went off without a hitch Friday night, and Saturday evening, all the guys stood around in the backroom of the chapel, waiting to go into the sanctuary and stand beside Gus as he took his wedding vows.

"Who would have thought that, less than a year ago, when Phoebe slapped Gus across the face for trying to get her into a compromising position at Logan's party, they'd be getting married?" Aaron stage-whispered to his brother, Owen.

"Who would have thought that you would be married to a feisty little girl from Guatemala less than three weeks after you met?" Owen replied.

"Wait, who got married?" That caught Gus's attention and inadvertently all the other guys' in the room.

"Aaron did." Their brother, Hayden, patted Aaron on the shoulder and smirked at Gus. "Our oldest brother beat us to the altar."

Aaron puffed up his chest and lifted his chin. "And I didn't even have to get her pregnant to convince her to marry me."

"Oh! Burn! He got you!" Jeers from around the room teased Gus. He stood there turning beet red.

"I did not get Phoebe pregnant on purpose," Gus grumbled through clenched teeth. "Besides, that's not exactly common knowledge."

They all looked around the room at one another. The four brothers, Alex, Jr., Alexander, Sr., and Prince Marcos nodded and shrugged as if to say, we all knew.

"I'm a little offended I didn't know until yesterday and had to find out from mom," Aaron said. "You could have warned your oldest brother."

"Not exactly the kind of thing you make an international phone call to admit." Gus looked down at the floor. "Imagine my embarrassment having to tell Mom and Dad."

"Son, no one's judging you," their dad said, then gave Aaron a pointed look.

"Shoot," Alex, Jr. said. "At least you *can* get your girlfriends and wives pregnant. I hope someday I'll regain the use of that particular part of my body." Alex placed his hands on the wheels of his wheelchair, and everyone grew quiet again.

"We all hope that too, son," Alexander, Sr. said, patting Alex on his shoulder. "For now, let's all pull ourselves together and get this show on the road. Gus's bride awaits."

"And her morning sickness won't kick in until tomorrow morning, so you should be able to have a fun night," Owen said with a smirk.

That caused the taunts to start up again, and they all teased Gus a few more times.

"Hey, guys, can I have a couple of minutes with my brothers and Alex?" Gus grew serious for a moment, glancing at Prince Marcos and Alexander, Sr.

"Sure, we'll give you some privacy," their dad said. "We need to get out there and help with the ushering anyway."

Their fathers left the room, and Gus led his brothers and Alex over to a little grouping of seats where they could sit down and be at eye level with Alex.

"I just wanted to thank you guys," Gus said. "The five of us are the only people who experienced the full trauma of our accident, and I just wanted to thank you all again for sticking together. I don't think I could have gotten through this past year without you."

"I know I couldn't have," Alex said.

"We pulled each other through the past year," Aaron said. "And things are only going to continue to improve. Alex, I think you'll eventually make a full recovery, and I'm pretty sure Ellen will stand beside you even if you don't. Owen, maybe you'll find a girl crazy enough to date you. And, Hayden, don't get the Princess Miranda pregnant."

"Are you kidding?" Hayden feigned a gasp. "I do not want to feel the wrath of her father. It's going to be hard enough to stand before the king of Madain Saleh and ask permission to marry his daughter."

"Good luck with that," Aaron said, then turned to Gus. "And seriously, man, you'll be a great dad. Things will all work out."

"On that note, let's go get Daddy Warbucks here married so he can give that baby mamma his last name and a small fortune as an inheritance. You did get a prenuptial agreement, right?" Aaron asked.

"Very funny." Gus stood, and the brothers followed his lead.

He held open the door for Alex to wheel through, then Aaron, Owen, and Hayden took their places at the front of the sanctuary. Alex followed in his wheelchair and stopped beside Gus as his best man.

At the last minute, Aaron and Gus each took an arm and helped Alex out of his chair while Owen pulled the wheelchair back and out of the way so Alex could be on his feet for the ceremony and photos. He could stand for a little while as long as he didn't try to walk.

A lot had changed in the past year, but a lot had stayed the same. The four brothers and their honorary prince, side by side in solidarity, lucky to be alive and ready to face the next phase in their lives.

Chapter Sixteen

Senator Alejandro and Captain Monroe

Krystina Stephenson, Alex's mom, had taken it upon herself to tuck Felicia under her wing and stay by her side the entire wedding and most of the reception since Aaron would be busy with the wedding party.

Aaron watched them from the head table, wishing he could be the one introducing his wife to all their friends and family. Sometimes they would point over toward Aaron and the person would smile and wave and congratulate Felicia.

Finally, when dinner was over and the cake had been cut and the wedding party was free to disperse, Aaron went to find his bride and then his grandfather.

"Oh, thank goodness," Felicia said when she was finally in Aaron's arms. "I thought I'd never get you back."

"You have me forever, my darling." Aaron leaned closer and lifted her chin delicately, afraid if he kissed his bride with too much passion, he'd end up sneaking her away somewhere and doing things that needed to wait until later that night. He forced himself to remember the kidnapped girls and lifted his gaze to search the room for his grandfather, Senator Alejandro Cohen.

They found the senator at a table with Aaron's cousin, Monroe, who was dressed in full uniform, having recently been promoted to the rank of Captain in the United States Army. He was receiving almost as much attention and congratulations as the bride and groom.

Monroe stood whenever someone approached to shake his hand or thank him for his service.

Aaron was surprised to find two open seats beside their grandfather, and he let Felicia sit closest to the senator while he tucked up behind her, practically wrapping her in a little cocoon of his loving arms.

"Greetings, my young prince," his grandfather said. "All grown up and brought your adorable wife to meet me." He held Felicia's hand between his own, a peaceful smile breaking through his political facade.

"Hola, Abuelo," Aaron said. "Esta es Felicia."

"My dear, welcome to the family," their grandfather answered in Spanish, taking Aaron's cue.

"She's sort of already part of the family," Aaron said. "Felicia is your brother, Santiago's, granddaughter."

"Well, how extraordinary."

"Grandpa, we need your help." Aaron heard the desperation in his own voice. "Some girls near where Felicia lives in Guatemala have been kidnapped from their refugee camp, and we believe they're being trafficked as sex slaves. We need to get the U.S. government involved somehow."

"You should talk to our cousin, Henry," Monroe interjected. "His position in the Army specializes in helping refugees."

"Really? I didn't know we had a cousin named Henry." Aaron was trying to mentally search back in their family tree. His paternal grandfather, Prince Benjamin, had only one son, his father, Prince Marcos. His maternal grandfather, Alejandro, had two children, his mom, Hazel, and her twin brother, Mateo, and their older brother, Lorenzo, who was Monroe's dad. He didn't have any other cousins that he knew of. "Are you talking about Alex's cousin?"

"Yes, Henry is Alexander's cousin." Monroe glanced across the room to where Alex was dancing with Ellen on his lap, on his wheelchair, in the middle of the dancefloor, cheek to cheek, swaying to the soft beat of a love song. "Son of Alexander's dad's brother, Frederick. He'd be, like, our second cousin twice removed or something weird like that. We'll just call him our cousin and be good."

"Is he here?" Aaron asked, looking around the room.

"He's on the dance floor, fighting off every eligible bachelorette in the reception hall. He's the guy in uniform."

"Another officer," Aaron said. "I'm impressed."

"Another captain, actually," Monroe corrected him.

"Double impressed," Aaron said. "Congratulations on your new commission, by the way."

"Thank you." Monroe nodded his head with subdued humility. He was the epitome of what every serviceman vowed when taking the oath to defend all enemies, foreign and domestic.

"Thank you, for your service. I'm honored to call you my cousin."

"Likewise, Your Highness."

"Now, now, none of that," Aaron said. "I abdicated my throne, remember?"

"Whatever. Once a spoiled, little prince, always a spoiled, little prince."

"Once a cocky, older cousin, always a cocky, older cousin."

"You know it." Monroe reached over for a fist bump, then stood and straightened his uniform. "I'll go drag our other cocky, older cousin away from his harem, and you can explain the situation to us like only civilians can. We'll put our heads together and see if we can't brainstorm some ways we can be of service."

Chapter Seventeen

Captain Henry Stephenson

"Tell me more about the situation in Guatemala." Army Captain Henry Stephenson pulled up a chair between Monroe and their grandfather, Senator Cohen, so that they could face Aaron and Felicia. He spoke in Spanish and directed his attention to Felicia.

"The problem is actually in Belize." Felicia seemed relieved to speak in her native language, but also to have everyone taking her seriously. "I live in a border town between Guatemala and Belize. Our two countries have been in a civil war for many years and the Mayans agreed to stop fighting in exchange for a reserved land for them to live.

"The reservation spans across both borders and neither country seems to want to claim jurisdiction of the reservation. When the girls started going missing on the Belizean side of the border, those of us in Guatemala just assumed that it was men in Belize stealing the girls. But when we went up there to talk to the Mayans, we found out the people stealing the girls were white men, possibly from America."

Both officers took a soft gasp at that revelation. Now maybe they understood why the United States needed to get involved.

"What is the Belizean government doing about it?" Monroe asked.

"So far they haven't done anything," Aaron said. "I'm not even sure they know what's going on. If they do, there are corrupt people within the government stopping them from accomplishing any sort of intervention on behalf of the girls."

"Where are the Americans taking the girls?" Henry asked.

"We think they're taking them to a port town called Belize City where they are either selling them or using them as sex slaves right there at the resort town."

"Well, my experience is with refugees," Henry said. "But I know of a nonprofit called Operation Freedom Warriors who help take down human trafficking rings. I'll try to get in touch with the people on the ground in Belize. Why don't I fly down there with you and assess the situation, and then we can go from there."

"Can you get the time off from the Army like that?" Aaron asked.

"Yes, I have some paid leave available right now, and we're not deployed so I can take a few days off."

Aaron had never known what it was like to depend on a paycheck. He wondered how hard that must be. He wished he could figure out a way to use his money in a more philanthropic manner. He would keep an eye open for his opportunity to be of service.

For now, the best way he could help is to rescue these young girls and bring them back to their families.

He was thankful to have Monroe and Henry assisting.

Part Two: Henry's Story

As told by Army Captain Henry Stephenson, son of Frederick Stephenson, grandson of Alexandria Cohen-Stephenson, great-grandson of Nicholas Cohen, great-great grandson of Levi Cohen. King Sayid, had recently passed away at the age of one hundred and six as the story begins...

Chapter Eighteen

Meeting Whitney

"My name is Whitney Olson. I'm the director of the aftercare program for Operation Freedom Warriors here in Belize. I understand you have some questions. How can I be of assistance?"

Henry was immediately tongue-tied, meeting the gaze of the beautiful, young humanitarian aid worker. Her tired eyes sat beneath a messy bun with strands of hair that had escaped and curled into natural tendrils haphazardly around her face. He wanted to tuck one of those stray hairs behind her ear, wrap his arms around her, and take all the pains of the world off her shoulders.

His distant cousin, and the expedition's financier, Prince Aaron Sayid, nudged his shoulder, waking him from his stupor.

"Hello, Ms. Olson. I'm Captain Henry Stephenson, U.S. Army." The minute Henry took Whitney's hand in his, a current of warmth traveled up his arm, and he couldn't let go.

Whitney must have felt the current also because her jaw dropped and her gaze lowered to their adjoined hands. Then she pulled her hand away suddenly and shook it out as if she'd experienced mild electrocution. She visibly gulped and directed her eyes elsewhere. "How can I help you, Captain?"

"We, actually, wanted to help you." Henry shook off his temporary daze. "We're trying to rescue the girls from the Mayan tribe at El Pilar." He wasn't sure if Whitney would even know where El Pilar was located. Heck, he had never been there either. He, Aaron, and Felicia had flown a private jet directly from New York to Belize City, where the Operation Freedom Warriors makeshift headquarters was located.

Dozens of other humanitarian aid workers milled about, leaning over large maps and schematics, talking on cell phones, and planning something. Henry only knew a little about the organization, that they rescued kids from child trafficking and may have insight into the missing girls from the reservation.

"Captain, we assist hundreds of girls and women who have been trafficked," Whitney said. "I couldn't possibly tell where all of them are from."

"Is there anyone who can?" Aaron butted in. "Someone has to talk to the girls after they're rescued, right? Don't you have to figure out where they were stolen from so that they can be returned to their families?"

"Many of the girls were sold into slavery *by* their families," Whitney explained. "We have to get them to safety first; treat any medical conditions they may have; get them cleaned up, fed, and clothed; find a safe place for them to sleep; and then start the process of figuring out where they're from."

"Can we talk to some of them? See if any of them are from El Pilar? Their families are terribly worried about them." Henry felt his hope diminishing.

"Three men? Not a chance!" Whitney took a step back with disdain, glancing between Henry, Aaron, and his driver, Joab. "You are the enemy. White American men in particular are the primary purchasers of sex slaves. Bringing one of you into our safe houses would be the opposite of helpful."

Aaron's bride, Felicia, stepped forward and spoke in Spanish. "What about me? Is there anything I can do to help?"

"Maybe." Whitney nodded, sizing her up and transitioning seamlessly to Spanish. "What is your nationality? Who are you?"

"I am Felicia Cohen-Sayid, married to Prince Aaron Sayid, a citizen of Guatemala, and descendant of Nicholas Cohen." Felicia was pulling out all the name recognition she could.

"Never heard of him." Whitney was not impressed. "How are you involved in all this?"

"I am sympathetic to the Mayan tribe who has been forced to live on a reservation these past years while dealing with the civil war between Belize and Guatemala." Felicia's impassioned speech showed her dedication to the cause. "When their women and children were stolen, I was among those who blamed the people of Belize. Finding out they were stolen by human traffickers was even more horrific than I could have imagined. I want to help rescue these girls."

"Ms. Olson, I'm Aaron Sayid, her husband. Felicia will work tirelessly to find these girls. Let her help you."

"Okay." Whitney nodded. "I'll see what I can do to get you involved. But you have to understand these things take time. This won't happen overnight."

"I understand." Felicia held her head high.

"And you're prepared to come with me right now?"

"Yes..." Felicia glanced back at her husband.

Aaron gripped her hand and nodded, encouraging her.

"Do you have identification with you? Including your passport?"

"Yes, I do."

"Why would she need her passport?" Aaron asked, his brow creased.

"We often get called upon to cross international boundaries, Mr. Sayid," Whitney said. "We go wherever we're needed."

Henry found it strange to hear anyone with the last name Sayid being called with the prefix mister. All his life the royal family had been referred to with their titles.

Just in the past few months since Aaron renounced his title and stepped down as crown prince and heir to the throne of the Kingdom of Madain Saleh, he had also insisted that people stop calling him Your Highness.

"Is there anything *we* can do to help with the rescue operations, Ms. Olson?" Henry asked, referring to himself and Aaron.

"As long as you're wearing *that* uniform, not likely, Captain." Whitney nodded toward him with longing in her eyes, almost as if wishing he wasn't. He technically wasn't wearing a uniform right that minute. More like jeans and an Army T-shirt, with dog tags around his neck.

"Why?" He gulped. "Since when is wearing a United States Army uniform a detriment to a humanitarian rescue?"

"You're limited by jurisdiction," she explained. "The sting operations we conduct are more than just rescuing refugees. We're taking down the criminals in the process. We work with local government jurisdictions within the country. These people have their own laws, and as long as you're representing the United States of America, you're bound by your oath."

"Doesn't that include all enemies foreign and domestic?" he challenged.

"Within your jurisdiction," she acknowledged. "You're on Belizean soil now, and you're not sanctioned to be here."

"She's got a point, Henry, I mean, Captain." Aaron cringed. "Sorry. Old habits die hard. You'll always be Henry to me. Alex's cousin."

"Thank you, Your Highness," Henry said. "I mean, Aaron. Sorry, you'll always be Crown Prince of Madain Saleh to me."

"Touché." Aaron held up a fist, and they bumped knuckles.

"You know, *you* could help out a lot, Aaron," Henry said. "Physically and financially. Not only do you have friends in some pretty high places, you have billions of dollars at your disposal."

"Is that what you need?" Aaron turned to Whitney like a puppy dog wagging his tail. "Do you need money? I have money. A lot of money. I can help."

"Are you for real?" Whitney's jaw dropped.

"I'm a billionaire prince without a throne or a purpose in life except to make love to my wife, and she's probably getting bored with me by now." Aaron winked at Felicia. "Put me to work."

Henry fought back a coughing fit, trying not to laugh as Felicia smacked Aaron in the stomach and growled the words, "Bored with you?" She smacked him again.

"Let me get this straight, you're offering me a willing volunteer to help identify our survivors, funding resources, friends in high places, and a newlywed willing to give up his wife to help?"

"Plus, an Army Captain willing to step down from his command if it means I can rescue these girls." Henry's voice grew husky as he lifted his chin to Whitney's gaze with a passion he didn't realize was inside him.

"Don't give up your commission too hastily, Captain," Whitney said with compassion in her voice. "We may need you right where you are."

Henry gulped and lowered his eyes, vulnerability entering his heart from the intensity of her gaze. "I'll do whatever you want me to do."

"Good to know." Her compassion shifted to something else. Anticipation, perhaps. Whitney turned to Felicia. "Say goodbye to your groom. I can't guarantee how soon you'll have the opportunity to... become *bored* with one another again."

Whitney winked at Henry as she turned and strode away. He kept his eyes on her on the other side of the room where she was talking to another aid worker and pointing in their direction.

Focusing on Whitney kept Henry from gagging at the sickly way Aaron and Felicia were kissing each other goodbye.

Bored. Henry chuckled to himself. Maybe someday Whitney would like to get bored with him.

Chapter Nineteen

I Don't Want the Ring

Whitney and the other aid worker walked in his direction, and Henry's stomach fluttered. The man's eyes were friendly and scanned back and forth between Aaron, Joab, and Henry. He smiled at Felicia, then extended his hand to Henry first.

Henry reassessed the man with his confident, firm handshake and realized almost immediately that he was not one of the aid workers; he was the man in charge of the whole operation.

"Greetings, gentlemen." The man nodded regally to Felicia and continued the conversation in Spanish. "And señora. Welcome to Operation Freedom Warriors. Thank you for your willingness to be of service. My name is Xavier Fulton. I'm the director of operations here."

"And founder of the non-profit, if I remember correctly," Henry said. "I've seen you on television."

"I do show my face on television occasionally." Xavier's eyes flickered over to Aaron, and he pursed his lips as if suppressing a smirk. "That's one of the reasons I'm the director rather than one of the undercover operatives. Some of us are too well known to blend in with society. Wouldn't you agree?" Xavier patted Aaron on the shoulder, and the young prince with the playboy reputation cleared his throat and lowered his eyes.

"I would agree," Aaron mumbled with humility. Henry found it hard to feel sorry for the kid since he was only compelled to be humble after a tragic accident that nearly took the life of his younger brother's best friend, Henry's cousin, Alex. Still, Aaron seemed to have changed his ways, and Henry needed to be more forgiving.

Henry also reminded himself that, moments ago, Aaron had pledged a small fortune to help the cause, as well as encouraged his young bride to devote her time exclusively to helping find the missing girls.

"Have you ever participated in donating large sums of money to any philanthropic ventures?" Xavier asked Aaron.

"No, sir." Aaron shook his head just slightly. "I'm sure our attorney can help us get some funds transferred to your organization. How much do you need right away? A couple million? I can get more. Heck, my wife's wedding ring's worth more than that." Aaron chuckled nervously.

"W-what?" All eyes were drawn to Felicia's left hand, which she held in front of her in shock. "I thought this was your grandmother's ring."

"Uh, well, my great-grandmother's actually. Princess Lyla Sayid. She found the ring at a jewelry bazaar in Dubai and tried to have it appraised in New York City." Aaron paused and shoved his hands into his pockets.

"Tried?" Henry asked, waiting for Aaron to explain.

"Apparently it's one of only a few surviving Le Vian diamond rings crafted in Persia in the late seventeen hundreds." Aaron spoke quickly as if not wanting to admit the truth.

"And..." Henry prompted. All of their eyes darted back and forth between the ring and Aaron's nervous fidgeting.

"And... the jeweler said the value is inestimable." Again, Aaron spoke very fast, then pulled his bottom lip between his teeth and glanced sheepishly at his wife. "Might not want to lose that."

"I can't wear this, Aaron!" Felicia slipped the ring from her hand and tried to give it back to her husband. "Donate the money to the organization."

"No, no, darling, you keep the ring. I'll get cash for the organization. Lots of it. Way more than the ring is worth. I promise." Aaron took the ring from her and tried to hold her hand to slip the priceless antique adornment onto her finger.

Felicia tucked her hands behind her back and shook her head like a child refusing to eat her broccoli.

"Darn it. I never should have told you," Aaron grumbled, then pleaded with his bride. "My mother wanted you to have this. The Princess Lyla would have wanted you to have this. Do you want the ring to sit in a safe or a museum? Xavier, tell her you don't want the ring. I'll transfer millions of dollars to your organization. Just tell Felicia you don't want the ring."

"Felicia, honey, I don't want the ring," Xavier said. "What would I do with a ring? I need money. Your husband's going to give me money. The ring belongs on your finger."

"We-we could s-sell the ring and do good things with the money." Tears ran down her face.

"My love, we *are* doing good things with my money. I will give away every penny of my money if you want me to. But please don't ask me to give away or sell this ring." Aaron held up the simplistic little diamond. "This has been passed down in my family for generations. I want us to pass it down to our children. And our children's children. Please? Will you *please* wear my great-grandmother's ring?"

"You promise you'll do good things with the rest of your money?" Felicia asked in a squeaky little-girl voice.

"I promise." Aaron turned to Xavier. "You'll help me do good things with my money, right?" Aaron nodded his head up and down as if to imply Xavier better answer in the affirmative.

"Of course." Xavier nodded with enthusiasm. "We will be able to rescue many, many girls with your husband's money."

"Like these Mayan girls we're trying to find," Aaron pointed out. "They're waiting for us to rescue them right now, and the longer we stand here talking about this ring, the longer they have to wait. Now, please, let me put the ring back on your finger, and let's go rescue those girls." Aaron held up the ring again.

"Okay," Felicia whispered. She held out her hand, and Aaron visibly relaxed as he slipped the ring onto his wife's finger and then pulled her into a hug.

While they were hugging, Felicia's phone rang with a video-chat call. She pulled back and glanced down at the screen. "It's my aunt Kisa." Felicia swiped her phone to turn on the chat window.

Before any of them had a chance to say hello, Kisa cried into the phone. "Two of the girls escaped! They ran through the woods from where the kidnappers have their base camp. They said the men are Americans, and the girls can lead us back to rescue the other girls! I'm already in the car, heading there now."

Henry glanced at his watch, then met Whitney's eyes and then Aaron's. "How long will it take to get to the reservation from here?"

"I have no idea!" Aaron said, holding up his hands as if in surrender.

Joab, Aaron's personal driver shook his head. "I'm not a local."

"I don't have a driver's license," Felicia said, shrugging.

"Where is this reservation?" Xavier asked as he pulled up a map on his phone.

"El Pilar," Felicia said.

"The archaeology site?" Xavier asked.

"Yes," Felicia answered. "The reservation is in the woods all around the archaeology site. They are well hidden."

Henry grumbled, "Not hidden enough apparently if their daughters have been kidnapped."

"We're only about two-and-a-half hours from there," Xavier said. "We can take my Jeep."

"We'll follow you in my Highlander," Joab said, holding up his keys.

Whitney put her hand on Henry's arm. "Captain, would you like to ride with Xavier and me, you know, so we can brief you about procedure."

"I would love that," Henry said, then cleared his throat, trying to hide the fact that her touch made his heart race. "Let's go rescue some girls."

Chapter Twenty

Operation Freedom Warriors

H enry clicked his seatbelt into place, settling into the middle seat of Xavier's Jeep since he had insisted Whitney sit in the front.

Although he wore jeans and a T-shirt, Henry felt as if he was starting into a mission without his weapons. Even with a backpack full of gear, including food, water, and supplies, he felt bare without forty pounds of Kevlar, a Beretta 9mm clipped to his belt, a knife in his boot, and an M16 rifle strapped on his back.

Walking unarmed into a fight was less than comfortable, but officer training had taught him that his most valuable tools were his brain and his radio. Maintaining communication with his team would keep him alive, and the guys in Operation Freedom Warriors had just become his team. Including the lovely Whitney Olson.

Whitney turned in her seat so that she was facing Xavier but frequently glanced back at Henry as if she couldn't help herself. Her professional facade kept slipping, and she would show a hint of a smile, then pull her features together again or glance down with a soft blush.

Dang, she was beautiful. Henry knew he needed to focus on the mission and finding the girls. He decided to ask about their organization and see if he could glean more information.

Xavier was a strong man of pure muscle. If Henry had to wager, he would guess some branch of the military or CIA. He pulled his Jeep out of the parking lot at the headquarters of his organization and headed for the Western Highway toward San Ignacio.

"Tell me more about what you do," Henry said. "And how I can help. Whitney mentioned that I should be careful not to jump ship because you may need me to hold my rank."

"She's right," Xavier said. "If these guys are indeed Americans, and we have a captain in the U.S. Army involved, we may need you to call in your higher-ups. On the reservation, even we don't have permission to do our job."

"When you say *do your job*," Henry asked, "what do you mean by that?"

"Operation Freedom Warriors is made up of dozens of retired and discharged military officers, ex-CIA, Homeland Security agents, and undercover officers," Xavier explained. "We took off our badges in order to remove the jurisdictional restrictions that were holding us back from doing our jobs with Freedom Warriors."

"Which is what?" Henry asked, wondering if he'd ever feel compelled to leave his commission.

"We conduct undercover sting operations to purchase children who are being sold into slavery."

"Wait, *purchase* children?" Henry gulped. "That's wrong."

"Someone's going to purchase them," Whitney said. "Better us than the pedophiles and sex traffickers."

"But you're still giving money to the criminals."

"Briefly," she explained. "And then we immediately arrest them."

"Why can't you just arrest them without purchasing children?"

"Because we wouldn't have any reason to arrest them," Xavier explained. "We couldn't prove that they had committed any crimes. Whereas if we purchase a child from them, then we know that they're selling children. We have proof, and we can put them in prison.

"If we can get close enough to the ringleader of the group, then we can rescue hundreds of children rather than just the one or two that we are purchasing. So it's important that we get close to them to get into their inner circle, not just be a onetime purchaser, but someone who's willing to bring other buyers down from America."

"Do you arrest the buyers also?" Henry asked.

"The buyers are all working for us. But at the time of the sting operation, yes, we allow everyone to be arrested so we can maintain our undercover status."

"So, you're able to do this more than once with the same group of individuals?"

"Yes, because we're trying to weed out the corrupt judges. So rather than posting bail, we allow them to go through the judicial system here in the country and learn what it takes to get them back out. Then we can discover who the corrupt judges are."

"How can this be happening right under our noses?" Henry asked. "How come it's Americans that are buying the children?"

"Child sex trafficking is more prevalent than you think it is," Xavier said. "This is the fastest growing criminal enterprise in the world."

"Really? More than drugs?" Henry had a hard time believing that.

"It's the fastest *growing*," Xavier clarified. "The difference is you can sell a bag of cocaine once, but you can sell a child ten or twenty times in a day."

"That's disgusting." Henry felt his stomach churn and wondered if they would need to pull the car over.

"Yes, it is. That's why we're doing what we're doing. It's modern day slavery. These kids are being used as a commodity. There are estimated thirty million slaves in the world today, and about ten million of them are children. About two million of them are sold into sex slave trade, and the rest of them are used as child labor."

"But if you are in slave labor," Whitney said, "it's just a matter of time before they use you for sex. Once they own you, you're a product, and they can do whatever they want with you."

"Is this something you have experienced?" Henry asked with compassion.

"Just as an aftercare humanitarian aid worker serving alongside survivors." Whitney's voice lowered and became emotional. "They tell some horrific stories."

"Are there slaves in the States too?" Henry asked. "Or is this mostly international?"

"People would like to think it's happening somewhere else," Xavier said. "But Americans are the biggest consumers of child pornography worldwide. Which means *we* are the market. *We* are the sex tourists."

"The United States is one of the top three destination countries," Whitney said.

"What do you mean by that?" Henry asked.

"The traffickers are trying to bring their slaves into the United States. They see the market and realize if they can get into our country, they can make a lot of money."

"So that Americans won't have to travel?" Henry guessed.

"That's right." Whitney nodded.

"Where is this happening? In big cities?"

"Well, in developing counties, where the infrastructure is not that great and the law enforcement struggle, you can see child sex slaves being sold on the street," Whitney said. "You're not going to see that in the United States. It's mostly online. We have warriors trained to infiltrate darknet groups to find kids."

"I've worked as an undercover operator in some capacity for almost nineteen years," Xavier said. "And I have bought and sold a child on every social media platform."

"No way."

"It starts on social media and then leads to private phone calls, then suddenly you're negotiating for a child."

"In person? No way."

"Yep."

"How did you originally get into this?"

"I started in the CIA, fighting terrorism. Then I was recruited to Homeland Security as an undercover operator. There's a lot of criminal activity at the ports of entry. I would have been busy for years fighting drug trades and human trafficking, but they called me in and told me they wanted to start a child trafficking unit. I had no idea child trafficking was a thing."

"No one wants to talk about it," Henry agreed.

"I didn't want anything to do with that. My wife agreed. We had just started a family. We didn't want to bring that darkness into our home. I didn't want to know what people are doing to kids."

"I don't blame you. I wouldn't want that either, and I don't even have a wife and kids... yet." Henry didn't mean to hesitate on the last word, somehow implying the possibility wasn't far off. Henry met Whitney's gaze. "What about you? Married? Kids?"

"Not yet," Whitney said softly.

Xavier didn't seem to notice their exchange nor the electricity hanging in the air between them and continued with his story. "I planned to turn down the job, and I was practicing my speech in the mirror, wondering how I was going to tell my boss, and my wife walks into the bathroom, and she's crying. She said she didn't sleep at all that night, and then she told me that for the same reason we didn't want you to do this was the reason we had to do this. Because we have children. If there really are millions of kids being trafficked, we can't allow this to happen."

"So, you started in the States?"

"Yes. Then, in 2006, the U.S. passed a law called the Adam Walsh Child Protection and Safety Act, which changed the statutory requirements for secondary sex traveler statutes."

"Meaning?"

"You can't travel to have sex with a child," Xavier said. "Prior to that, we had to prove a perpetrator had the intent to have sex with a child while standing on U.S. soil."

"That's impossible to prove," Henry said.

"Prior to 2006, we had zero prosecutions," Xavier said. "But the Adam Walsh Child Protection and Safety Act changed the law, so we don't have to prove the perpetrator was thinking about sex with a child while in the States. Now all we have to prove is that he left the States and that he committed the act. If we can prove *that,* we can hold him accountable as if he committed the act on our soil, and we can put him in jail in the States. Homeland Security put together a team and basically said, okay, guys, go out and find Americans who are doing this."

"But how do you know where to go to find these guys?" Henry asked.

"They sent me to undercover school to teach me how to be a pedophile, how to think like one, how to talk like one. I became an undercover operator and because I speak Spanish, they sent me mostly into Latin America, Guatemala, Mexico, Costa Rica, the Caribbean, Colombia. Once I get overseas, I can basically sit on the beach, and th e traffickers come to me. It's like they know that's what I'm there for."

"What do you mean? Sit on the beach?"

"Trafficking is so prevalent that they expect an American guy sitting on the beach alone is waiting for them to come offer what they have for sale."

"Which is?"

"Usually young girls. Preteens or early teens."

"Are you talking prostitution? Of little girls?" Henry gulped, knowing his nausea had nothing to do with the bumpy roads.

"Yep."

Henry balled his fists. He had seen some horrible things in the world, but imagining little girls having their innocence stolen in such a way was more than he wanted to envision.

"Hey, we can stop talking about this if you need." Whitney's soft voice pierced through Henry's shell, and he met her gaze. Her compassion was probably what kept her pushing through this job.

"No... I need... to hear this." Henry spoke through clenched teeth. "I need to know the truth so I can help stop this from happening to anyone else. Keep talking." Henry sat up straight, forced back his emotions, and put on his game face.

"Anyway, I don't want to just meet with the pimp on the beach. I want to get to know his boss and his boss's boss. You know what I mean?"

"Sure..."

"So, we put together this whole plan where we want to bring a group of guys down from the States, and I convince them to get a party together."

"And they fall for that?"

"Oh yeah, they do these all the time."

"All the..." Henry forced back his emotions and swallowed hard. "Keep going."

"I have to become friends with these guys, and they're showing me pictures on their phone and they've got ten-year-old girls, and I'm smiling and pretending. My stomach's churning, and I want to reach across and strangle this guy but I know I'll never find the kids if I do."

"Do you ever worry about becoming a pedophile after looking at all those pictures?"

"Actually, it's just the opposite," Xavier said. "If anything, you become less interested in sex. I mean, not to divulge too much information, but my poor wife. I have to go through a period of desensitization just to come back to the real world after an op."

Henry decided to change the subject after that very awkward question. "How did you transition from meeting these jerks on the beach to quitting your job and starting a nonprofit?"

"Remember how I said that we had to follow jurisdiction rules and laws when we're representing the government?" Xavier met Henry's gaze in the rearview mirror. "I was in deep with these guys and we were running out of budget. We couldn't find an American involved, but we were about to intercept about a hundred kids. And the order was given that we were out of money and I had to come home."

"You went all that way for nothing?"

"I went all that way and found a hundred kids."

"But you couldn't arrest the guys because there weren't any Americans?"

"Not working for the United States government." Xavier shook his head.

"What did you do?" Henry leaned forward and put his elbow on his knee, completely engrossed in Xavier's bravery.

"I took off my badge."

"Just like that?"

"Well, I talked to my wife first. She said, do it. We'll figure out a way to feed our family. God will provide. Save those kids." Xavier's facade broke and his voice cracked.

"And you saved the kids?"

"We saved the kids."

"But not your job?" Henry guessed.

"We started the nonprofit."

"And the rest is history?"

"Not quite. For that op we already had the local government involved. We didn't have that kind of relationship with other governments. We won't go into a foreign country unless we have the local law enforcement involved, and until we have the aftercare program in place."

"Which is where you come in?" Henry nodded to Whitney.

"I'm in charge of the aftercare program." Whitney nodded.

"So, you're in charge of the hundred kids after they're rescued?"

"Things are a little more complicated than that," Whitney said.

"The aftercare is the most important part," Xavier said. "More than half the time there's not a family member at home waiting for their missing child with open arms. Some families are part of the problem. There are families who are so poor they're selling their kids into slavery."

"The first thing we do," Whitney said, "is to let the kids know they're safe and we're not the bad guys. Because they've just witnessed a raid, and people getting arrested, and chaos and shouting, they're traumatized. They don't know what's going on. We have the aftercare team right there on the ground as the raid is happening."

"How could a parent sell their child?"

"I think some people are just so poor and desperate, selling themselves and their children becomes part of the culture, generational. Parents tell the kids, this is what I had to do when I was your age, so this is what you're going to do. And that's part of the problem. When something becomes culturally accepted, the laws reflect that as well. We can't help a country until they establish laws making that illegal."

"If I'm understanding this correctly, we have more than one problem," Henry said. "We've got the people selling kids for sex, but we've also got the pedophiles paying for sex."

"The guys don't even have to be paying for sex for us to arrest them. Even looking at child pornography is illegal, and we'd like to catch them *before* they become a contact offender."

"What's a contact offender?" Henry asked.

"Someone who is actively seeking sexual interaction with a child," Xavier explained. "Usually child pornographers will eventually want to take action, and that's when they become a contact offender."

"How many of these guys do you think there are?"

"Well, if there are two million children in sex slavery, consider what kind of number justifies that demand."

"Switching topics for a minute," Henry stopped them. "You don't normally have a billionaire prince walk up and hand you a couple million dollars. How do you get enough money to do these raids?"

"We have a few big donors, plus fundraisers. We never have enough money though. Although we now have law enforcement units in twenty-six countries, we can't keep up with the demand. With each new request for assistance, we have to evaluate whether that country is able to handle the stress of taking on this magnitude. We can give them all the tools and training, but they have to have the infrastructure to sustain the program. With limited resources, we have to go wherever we'll be able to make the biggest difference."

"For today, let's go make a difference for a couple of girls on a Mayan reservation in Belize." Henry felt a sense of peace even after hearing those horrific details. If he could save even one child, it was worth the risk to his life and his job.

Chapter Twenty-One

We're Not Afraid to Fight

Henry barely waited for Xavier's Jeep to stop in the tourist parking lot at the archaeological site of El Pilar before opening the side door. He swung his pack over his shoulders and clipped the chest strap in place. Joab's Highlander pulled up beside the Jeep and Aaron, Felicia, and Joab climbed out. They headed into the woods past a no-trespassing sign.

The trail was barely evident until they were upon the unmarked trailhead, and only if a person knew what to look for. Felicia had mentioned that the tribe was well hidden. At least from this direction, she was correct.

A Hispanic woman in her late twenties hurried toward them up the path. "Thank goodness. I thought you'd never get here." Without introductions, the woman kissed Joab, hugged Felicia, and hurried back the way she had come.

Felicia turned to Henry and explained the woman was her aunt Kisa. They all followed Kisa another few hundred feet until the forest opened into a small clearing not much larger than a basketball court.

All around the clearing, homes had been built in such a way that they were almost hidden in plain sight. The forest shrouded a village that seemed much larger than Henry expected. Now that he knew what to look for, he realized there were homes dotted throughout the woods as far as he could see.

Several tribal women approached and spoke hurried Spanish intermingled with another language Henry didn't recognize. Again, with no introductions, Henry and the rescue party followed the women. The paths through the forest were more pronounced here, as if worn down by countless feet.

Finally, they arrived at an area that was bustling with activity. Dozens of teenage boys seemed to be arguing with their parents and tribal leaders in that same garbled mix of Spanish and the native language Henry didn't recognize. He tried to pick out Spanish words in an attempt to understand. *Sister. Going. Do nothing. Fight. Retaliate.* None of it made sense.

Felicia seemed to understand the language and spoke with several of the tribe members. She turned toward them, and her eyes searched for Whitney. "You need to come talk to the girls," Felicia said in Spanish.

Whitney stepped forward without hesitation and followed Felicia and several other women into a nearby home.

Henry and Xavier approached Aaron and Joab where they were speaking with several men.

"What's going on?" Henry asked.

"The boys want to retaliate," Aaron said, turning to a man who must have been a tribal leader. "They want to break the treaty and go after the kidnappers."

Most of the teenagers stopped arguing and turned their attention to the newcomers.

Henry spoke directly to the tribal leader. "I am Captain Henry Stephenson with the United States Army. How can we help you rescue your daughters?"

"Tell our boys not to fight!" The man spoke in impassioned Spanish, pointing behind him with exasperation. "We took an oath. We will not break the treaty."

One of the young men stepped forward. "Kids in our generation were babies when you made that agreement. *We* did not take an oath, father. We will not be violating your treaty."

"Besides, those are our sisters out there," another boy said.

"My girlfriend." With tears fighting to surface, another young man lifted his chin. "We were to be married next week."

Henry's heart broke for these boys. He understood the need to help, to do something, to rescue the girls. This was inherent in men to be protectors. "Do we know how many kidnappers there were?"

"Fewer than ten, the girls said." The tribal leader's shoulders sagged in defeat, or exhaustion. "They weren't sure exactly how many."

"Do you know how the girls escaped?" Xavier asked.

"They... got the men drunk... and..." The tribal leader lowered his voice. "You can probably figure out the rest."

All the boys and men within earshot quieted or grumbled or shuffled their feet. No one wanted to voice what they all knew happened.

"They snuck out of the men's tents and ran through the night," the tribal leader continued, "and all through the following day."

"They must be exhausted," Henry said.

"We have insisted they rest tonight, and a search party can leave at first light, allowing the girls to lead the way."

"Who all is going on the search party?" Henry raised his hand to encourage others to volunteer, inadvertently offering himself as a volunteer also. He looked around at the men and boys.

Every one of the teenage boys raised their hands, lifted their chins, and stepped forward. Some called out affirmations.

"We're not afraid to fight."

"My mother's been crying for days since my sister was kidnapped."

"My mother also."

"Our fathers have been obedient to their oath. We need to defend them."

"What kinds of supplies do you have?" Henry asked. "You each need food and water, and basic necessities, enough for three days. Plus, we need to bring enough provisions for the women, our guides, and the girls we plan to rescue. Do you have any weapons?"

"We have hunting rifles, compound bows, and hunting knives." The boy who was planning the wedding stepped forward, then turned and took on a leadership role for his younger friends. "Guys, bring all weapons here to the community center, along with all ammunition, and start packing supplies. Let's take inventory of what we have and figure out what else we need."

As if accustomed to taking orders from this young man, the teenagers scattered, already on task. Impressive.

"What's your name, son?" Henry asked the boy. "And how old are you?"

"My name is Machudo, and I am nineteen."

"Consider yourself my second in command."

"Yes, sir, Captain Henry. I won't let you down."

"Let's go rescue your future bride." Henry placed his hand on the young man's shoulder, and they looked one another in the eye. Henry had never seen such courage in all his years in the Army. He vowed in that moment he would put his life on the line for these boys.

Chapter Twenty-Two

I'm Riding with You

"You've been busy." Whitney wiped her brow and sighed, the weight of the world on her shoulders. The community center where Henry and the teenage boys had gathered and organized supplies in preparation for their early departure the following morning was strewn with overflowing backpacks, weapons, and provisions.

Whitney had been holed up with the Mayan girls most of the evening and was finally done for the night. Henry handed her a recently boiled and filtered bottle of water and pulled out a chair for her.

She took the proffered water bottle and sank onto the folding chair. Propping her feet onto another chair, she leaned back and drank heartily. "Thanks, I needed this." She recapped the bottle and closed her eyes.

"I know you just sat down, but you won't want to get too comfortable. Aaron and I arranged for you and Xavier to each have a hotel room at the resort in San Ignacio, compliments of his highness."

"Let me get this straight." Whitney opened one eye but didn't lift her head from where it slumped on the back of her chair. "That kid with you is seriously a prince?"

"Uh... yeah." Henry pulled up a chair, turned it backward, and straddled the seat so he could lean on the back and face Whitney. He glanced to the side to where Aaron and Felicia were sitting on similar folding chairs across the room. Not sure how much Aaron could hear, Henry spoke quietly. "Aaron sort of abdicated his throne, but I'm not sure it was ever really his to begin with. Another civil war on the opposite side of the world I'm glad I don't have to fight. I suppose if the people in Madain Saleh were kidnapping and raping young girls I'd be more concerned."

"Where the heck is Madain Saleh?" Whitney opened both eyes.

That caught Aaron's attention and his head lifted. Henry spoke a little louder, knowing there was no reason to try to hide his snarky response. "Somewhere in the Arabian desert. I don't know. The country barely exists anymore."

"I resent that," Aaron called from across the room.

"Go live in the desert then, Your Highness," Henry called back.

"I'm good. I'll stay here in the jungle where the heat retains its humidity."

"This is a forest, not a jungle, but good try," Whitney teased, getting in on the banter.

"Are you guys about ready to head to the resort?" Aaron stood and helped Felicia off the chair where she'd been sitting. "My bride and I are exhausted."

"Is that what you're calling it now?" Whitney smirked. "Earlier today you were bored and now you're exhausted."

"Yes, well, we haven't had a chance to be bored yet today, so let's get a move on."

"Are all newlyweds this sappy?" Whitney asked.

"I don't know," Henry teased back. "I'll let you know a few days after our wedding."

"Oh, you will, will you?" Whitney laughed. "Help me up so you can take me to your hotel. And don't get any ideas about which room is yours."

"Why, Ms. Olson, I'm shocked at your insinuations." Henry helped her to a standing position and fought the urge to wrap his arms around her. "You think just 'cause we flirted in a Jeep for three hours that I'm going to invite you to my hotel room? What kind of a man do you think I am?"

"Think? Or hope?" She raised her eyebrows and smirked.

The sound that emerged from the back of Henry's throat was almost a tiger purr. He met her gaze and spoke low enough for her ears only. "Ya know, after we get all done rescuing teenagers, you and I should go out to dinner or something and continue this conversation."

"Something to look forward to, Cap'n Henry." Whitney winked at him and walked away, shifting to Spanish to ask Felicia if she's coming with the rescue team the following morning.

"Wait." Henry hurried to catch up to the ladies as they walked through the door, out into the near blackness of late evening, in the middle of a forest shrouded with a thick canopy and noticeable lack of modern electricity. He was glad they were heading to a hotel. "Are *you* coming on the trek with us?"

Whitney turned to face him. "Uh, yeah." The word sounded more like *duh*, and Henry felt silly for asking. She was the aftercare aid worker in charge of treating the girls once they'd been rescued.

"Right. Of course, you are. What was I thinking?"

"I dunno. What *were* you thinking?" Whitney looked him up and down with flirty eyes.

"I'm thinking you're a little punch drunk, and we need to get you a good night's rest so you can save the world tomorrow."

"Saving the world is so overrated." Whitney turned and followed Aaron and Felicia out to the trail where they met up with Xavier, Joab, and Kisa.

"Who's riding with whom?" Joab held up his car keys.

Kisa was the first to respond. "I'll leave my car here and ride back with you and my niece and her prince charming."

"You might want to drive fast, Joab," Henry stage-whispered. "Who knows what might happen with two bored newlyweds in the back seat of your Highlander."

"I'm never going to live that down, am I?" Aaron pinched the bridge of his nose.

"Nope." Henry popped the P in emphasis.

"Fine then, I'll own it," Aaron said, turning to Joab. "Might want to drive fast."

"I'm a driver for a living," Joab said. "I can handle fast. Besides, the faster I drive us to the hotel, the faster I can get Kisa alone for a few minutes of our own."

Henry turned to Xavier and Whitney. "I'm riding back to the hotel with *you guys*."

They all chuckled and turned on flashlights so they could navigate the uneven forest path up the hill to El Pilar.

Chapter Twenty-Three

Vigilantes

Refreshed from a decent night's sleep in one of the finest suites at the San Ignacio Resort, Henry repacked his backpack, focusing his energy on this mission as if on assignment from his superior officers. He had taken the time the previous evening to train the teenagers in some basic reconnaissance skills and strategies.

The poorly organized and cocky teenagers were under the mistaken impression that knowing how to shoot a brocket deer with a compound crossbow or stalk and kill a gibnut qualifies them for tactical guerrilla warfare.

Henry saw disaster ahead if he didn't take action. He divided them into teams of four and assigned each team a sergeant. Not knowing the kids in advance, he operated on instinct, eyeballing which of the four boys was most likely to take charge.

He made sure each team had at least one hunting rifle or compound crossbow. Thankfully, every young man owned a hunting knife and knew how to spear an iguana from twenty meters away.

Henry grouped two teams of four into squads and assigned a staff sergeant, then pulled together two squads into platoons and designated a lieutenant to each platoon. Those two platoons made up his company of thirty-two hotheads ready to take on the world and rescue their girlfriends and sisters.

What could have been a logistical nightmare quickly organized into his dream team of soldiers. Inexperienced soldiers, but soldiers, nonetheless. Confidence replaced cockiness, and the boys were motivated by love and duty.

Each squad was in charge of one woman or teenage girl, performing the double duty of bodyguards and carriers of provisions. He refused to ask the exhausted girls to carry any weight. They should have been convalescing.

Once the remaining girls were rescued, one platoon would escort the girls home immediately and the other platoon would stay and take down the kidnappers.

Machudo was designated as Henry's first lieutenant and asked to watch everything he did. If something happened to Henry, Machudo needed to take charge. No pressure there.

This could work.

Or this could be a disaster.

By the end of the day, they'd know one way or the other.

Henry swung his organized backpack onto his shoulders, clicked the chest strap into place, and then headed out of his suite to find the lovebirds and humanitarian aid workers.

"You look battle-ready." Whitney's voice welcomed him when he stepped into the hallway from his hotel room.

Henry turned to find her leaning against the wall, wearing sturdy clothing and a backpack of her own. "You as well. Where the heck did you get the change of clothes?"

"We have gear in the Jeep all the time in case we have to pick up and move in a hurry."

"Your organization is impressive."

"Keep those bars on your shoulder, Captain," Whitney said. "We need you right where you are."

"Yeah, well, if I lead a company of amateur soldiers into battle, I may not have a choice. Those bars might be ripped from my shoulder the minute I step on U.S. soil."

"We'll cross that bridge when or if that happens," Whitney said. "Let's hope it doesn't come to that, but you know where to look for us if you find yourself out of a job."

"I'd be honored to serve at your side." Gone was the flirting from the night before. This was a serious conversation and declaration of commitment to one another. Henry hoped he lived through the next few days so he could explore the potential relationship he felt developing between himself and Whitney Olson.

Before the discussion could get any deeper, Kisa and Joab emerged from a suite down the hall, Felicia and Aaron from another, and Xavier from the third. His team of vigilantes headed down the hotel elevator, intent to make use of the full service breakfast before driving back up the mountain to lead a team of young men into the wilderness guided by two frightened girls.

What could possibly go wrong?

Chapter Twenty-Four

We Are Still the Enemy

T he makeshift company had a total of twelve cell phones between the thirty-eight of them. Not enough. But each team of four had a cell, plus one for each of the leaders, Henry, Whitney, Xavier, and Machudo.

All twelve cell phones were linked with coms and GPS tracking, and Prince Aaron acted as ground control at the reservation. He had clear instructions about whom to call if anything should go wrong with the mission.

The plan was to have Xavier and Whitney lead one platoon back to the reservation, along with the kidnapped girls once they'd been liberated.

Henry planned to keep Machudo and an entire platoon with him to suppress and take the criminals into custody. The kidnappers needed to be kept alive to conduct a full interrogation and learn the location of the remaining human trafficking ring.

Although twenty-four girls had been kidnapped from the tribe, they were unaware how many girls were still in the area, and how many of them had already been trafficked to another location.

Henry's superior officers would eventually be notified of his involvement, but he hoped to get a slap on the wrist and demotion rather than a direct order to stand down.

Coming home after rescuing twenty-four kidnapped Mayan girls would go a long way to receiving forgiveness for subordination. Coming home with dozens of wounded or slain teenage boys would not. He needed this mission to be a success. Failure was not an option.

A real concern was losing their path back to the kidnappers' base camp. Thankfully, the two young guides remembered how to traverse the woods leading to the makeshift footpath cut by their abductors. Less than a mile from the reservation, they arrived at an actual trail that the kidnappers had been using to brazenly sneak close enough to skirt the unmarked boundaries of the reservation. From that point on, all the company needed was to keep marching and follow that path.

Another challenge was the unknown time frame between leaving that morning and arriving at the base camp. The two girls who escaped ran as fast as they could to get away from the kidnappers. Even with a head start of several hours, the girls knew their captors could easily overtake them if they stopped to rest. They had arrived at the reservation exhausted, dehydrated, filthy, and terrified, yet less than twenty-four hours later they were trekking back to the very place from which they'd fled.

Adrenalin only lasted an hour into the trek, and the teenagers dragged for a few hours. To their credit, they never stopped marching. They barely paused long enough to step behind a tree, and they marched through lunchtime, satisfied with protein bars and sips of water.

At one point in the afternoon, the youngest and smallest of the two teenage girls climbed onto the back of her older brother and clung to him like a monkey. Henry wondered if the connection was almost a relief for the brother as well as his little sister. The physical aspect of holding a person in your arms after losing them is powerful and healing. The move even seemed to boost morale for others in the group, especially those young men whose sisters and girlfriends had been ripped from their lives. They were motivated by the desire to hold their loved ones as well.

When evening fell and darkness shrouded the trail, Henry ordered a much-needed break. Most of the kids sat on the ground to eat and rest their legs, and some even rested their heads on each other's laps, closing their eyes for a quick nap. Henry and Machudo each took a protein bar with them and kept walking. They promised not to engage the enemy until the full company arrived as backup, but at least they could give a heads-up to the other leaders how many more hours were left to travel.

Machudo showed a determination unlike anyone Henry had seen. He loved this girl he was trying to rescue and nothing else in the world mattered other than finding her.

Henry wondered how that would feel to love a woman so strongly. His mind played back to the moment twenty-seven hours ago when he'd clasped hands with Whitney. Could he someday fall in love with a woman like her? Could she ever love a man like him? The possibility was worth pursuing. She seemed interested. And he was definitely interested in her.

After two more hours of walking, Henry and Machudo seemed to sense a change at the same time and their footfalls paused. Listening to the sounds of the night, they held perfectly still. Hearing nothing but insects and the occasional soft coo of a night bird, they continued forward slowly and with softer strides, keeping to one side of the trail.

Within ten minutes, Henry smelled the unmistakable whiff of a campfire, and he led Machudo off the path and into the cover of the forest. Creeping forward with controlled footing, they climbed a rise and lowered to their bellies, gaining a vantage point over a makeshift campsite that closely resembled the one the girls had described.

Henry sent a quick text to Whitney relaying the time and GPS location of their whereabouts. She and Xavier would pass along the message to Aaron and the tribal leaders back on the reservation. Communication was the key to their survival.

For almost an hour, they waited and watched, taking inventory of the numbers of tents, visible men, campfires, and weapons. There was no evidence of any girls, but that didn't mean the girls weren't hidden in the tents. There was one SUV designed for off-roading and covered in fresh mud

.

The men didn't seem to be prepared for, or expecting, an ambush. They sat around the fires, talking, eating, drinking, smoking cigarettes—relaxed—not a care in the world. Good. Henry and his company would have the element of surprise to their advantage. But only if the rest of the company could approach the campsite without making any noise.

From texts he'd received from Whitney, he knew that Xavier and one squad of eight had taken off at a full run from their last position in an attempt to provide immediate backup for Henry and Machudo.

Almost exactly one hour from when Henry and Machudo had called in their location, Henry received word from Aaron that the GPS signal from Xavier's squad was approaching Henry's position and that Aaron had already notified Xavier to halt progression and wait for Henry to meet them.

He and Machudo crept back down the rise and cautiously approached the trail where they came upon Xavier's squad. Without preamble, all eleven guys slipped into the woods and gathered close to share intel.

"There's a stone ridge to the right of the path where we have a vantage point." Henry spoke low and fast. "The ridge must have been a structure at one time, because the four corners are symmetrical. We haven't seen any girls, but we've seen six men, all armed, none on high alert. They seem to be winding down for the night, and if we wait another half hour or so, they will mostly be in their tents and we'll have the element of surprise on our sides. Let's lay low on the ridge, watching until more backup arrives. We don't want to go in unprepared. Machudo, take one team back to the ridge where we just were. Xavier and I will climb the ridge on the opposite side with the other team. We can talk strategy as we watch. Do not engage the enemy without my command. Is that clear?"

The eight teenagers nodded with wide eyes and in terror that they'd come this far and were within sight of the targets.

"Once the rest of the company arrives, we'll skirt the campsite and take up positions around the tents and near the road leading out of the campsite. There's a large SUV over there with fresh mud on the tires. We don't want them to get away, but we also need them alive. We have to find a way to get eyes on the location of the girls, and the rescue needs to be fast, in and out."

"There was a clearing back there about half a mile," Xavier said. "The young guides and one team will wait there while Whitney and the rest of the company join us here. She wants to be on the ground immediately when we get the girls into our custody. She and one team will help with the rescue so that the girls can see their brothers immediately rather than you and me. As white men, we are still the enemy in their eyes. We don't want the girls fleeing from us."

"Yeah, that would be bad." Henry nodded, then looked around. "Okay, everyone understand their orders? Let's move."

Chapter Twenty-Five

For Luck

T he two teams watched from the ridge for another forty-five minutes before Henry received word that the remaining members of the company had stopped at the clearing. One team of four would stay in the clearing with the two girls who had guided them this far while two squads of eight each, plus Whitney, would arrive to help rescue the remaining girls.

Each of the seven teams would have their assignments. One team would protect the entrance to the trail, one would surround the truck and slash the tires to prevent anyone from leaving. One team would be in charge of protecting Whitney and herding the rescued girls toward the footpath leading back to El Pilar. The other four teams would simultaneously attack the four tents, focusing on incapacitating the kidnappers without killing them. Henry, Xavier, and Machudo would be in charge of the raid.

After the girls were secured, Xavier and Whitney would take one full platoon plus the rescued girls and hightail back to El Pilar, only stopping if absolutely necessary.

Henry, Machudo, and the other platoon of sixteen boys would stay and take command of the kidnappers. The boys were instructed to wound the kidnappers in their right arms since there was a statistical probability that the men would be right-handed. Next, they were to immobilize the men by shooting or stabbing their legs.

This could work.

Could being the operative word.

When Whitney and her two squads of eight boys came into view, a physical weight lifted from Henry's shoulders. He met her gaze, and Whitney took a deep sigh. They were both relieved to see each other. She strode to her boss, Xavier, gave him a quick hug, then came to Henry and hugged him as well. Then she unexpectedly laced her fingers with his and whispered, "Hi."

Henry squeezed her hand in recognition of her presence and then started giving instructions. The boys were told to memorize the lines, "We're here to rescue you. Follow the white woman."

Whitney had worn a white shirt that seemed to glow in the moonlight. In addition to her white skin, her bright white shirt would leave no doubt in the girls' minds who the boys were pointing to.

As the teams made ready to enter the campsite, potentially exposing themselves to the enemy, Henry whispered to Whitney, "After you leave with the girls, I won't see you for a few hours. I just wanted to remind you that I have every intention of taking you out on a date very soon."

"I'm going to hold you to that," she whispered back, then turned to face him. "Stay safe, Captain Henry Stephenson."

"You as well, Whitney Olson."

Whitney lifted her heels and rose to kiss his cheek. "Good luck."

"Oh, honey, I'm going to need more than that for luck." Henry pulled her close and pressed his lips to hers in a goodbye kiss not knowing how soon they'd be reunited. When Henry tried to release her from his arms, Whitney pulled him closer and offered him one more kiss, this time with a bit more passion. If he died in battle, that kiss would be his last thought on earth.

They stepped apart and straightened their packs, preparing to leave the safety of the woods and enter the campsite. Henry hoped this plan would work, because he had someone very special to look forward to.

Chapter Twenty-Six

Trapped

Even though they thought all the men were in tents for the night, those first tentative steps into the campsite made Henry's heart race. He was glad to have spent several hours in reconnaissance before entering this space blind.

A small campfire smoldered in the center of the campsite, which seemed to be the remains of a city square. The river to the north was closer than he'd realized but he didn't think they'd be affected by it. What looked to be a citadel loomed on the other side of the campsite, which could serve as a place to hole up and become a stronghold if necessary.

The first team of boys crept carefully along the edge of the campsite toward the truck. They each stabbed their hunting knife into a truck tire, then tucked themselves into the surrounding forest near the road leading to San Ignacio. The four teams assigned to attack the tents simultaneously separated and skirted the edges of the campsite on the north and south sides, effectively surrounding the four tents. Once all four teams were in position, Henry, Xavier, and Machudo each took one tentative step into the campsite and waited.

Nothing.

They took another step.

Still no response from any of the tents nor from anywhere else in the campsite.

The tents each only had one opening, all facing in toward the fire, all flaps shut.

Henry gave the sign and all four teams advanced quickly to the tents, surrounding them. In a flurry of confusion, the boys used hunting knives to slit through the backs of the tents, not bothering with the front flaps.

Multiple hunting rifles fired off almost simultaneously, girls screamed, and men swore.

All around him, Henry heard the boys calling out in Spanish, "We're here to rescue you. Follow the white woman."

Girls began scurrying away from the tents, most of them clutching some sort of clothing or blanket, none of them wearing shoes. One girl was completely naked. One of the boys near Whitney quickly removed his shirt and draped it around the naked girl, offering her some comfort and protection.

Only eight girls were recovered.

Henry's heart sank, knowing the others had already been taken farther down the line to the trafficking ring in Belize City. He caught Machudo's attention from twenty feet away.

Machudo shook his head with sadness in his countenance. His girlfriend wasn't among the eight.

Within minutes of cutting open the tents, all eight girls, Whitney, and an entire platoon of amateur soldiers had disappeared down the path toward El Pilar. The girls would be offered immediate care. Whitney had brought shoes, hoodies, sweatpants, food and water, enough for all twenty-two missing girls. Only eight would be needed.

Taking the men into custody was not so easy. Although unprepared for the attack, some of them partially dressed, and all of them wounded by the boys' hunting rifles, they were larger and more experienced in a fight. Seventeen teenage boys who were shaken and scared were no match for six hardened criminals. The boys had no idea what to do. This was a mistake.

Henry had two choices; retreat or kill the men. They couldn't retreat down the footpath back toward El Pilar because they needed to lead the men away from the girls. That meant they needed to retreat toward the citadel. But first they had to give all they could.

Most of the boys had already lost their knives when throwing them at the men or stabbing them. There was only one hunting rifle for each team of four. They were unarmed, untrained, and terrified. There was only one real choice.

"To the citadel, now!" Henry yelled, and all seventeen teenage boys ran to the far end of the campsite. None of them were wounded in their legs, and they ran hard.

All of the kidnappers had at least one wound but none of them were incapacitated. The men also had found their weapons, and shots were fired. None of them hit their mark, and all seventeen boys made it through the entrance to the citadel and up the switchback stairs. Two of them used their rifles to shoot at the kidnappers.

The citadel was designed so that the enemy trying to climb the stairs would be sitting ducks for the boys above. The men would have been stupid to attempt an attack, even if they weren't injured.

The boys were safe for now.

But they were trapped.

Hemmed in by the sheer cliff down to the Belize River on the north and the kidnappers just out of shooting range with the hunting rifles, the boys could hold their position within the crumbling stronghold, but for how long? Even if they called back the platoon that had left to escort the girls back to the reservation, there weren't enough soldiers. Although not outnumbered by the enemy, young boys were no match for grown men who likely had unlimited ammunition and no motivation to keep the boys alive.

With dwindling supplies, and few options, Henry locked eyes with Machudo, hoping to convey a confidence that didn't exist in his heart. He pulled out his cell phone and connected immediately.

"Aaron, time to call in reinforcements."

Part Three: Monroe's Story

As told by Army Captain Monroe Cohen, son of Lorenzo Cohen, grandson of Alejandro Cohen, great-grandson of Nicholas Cohen, great-great grandson of Levi Cohen. King Sayid, had recently passed away at the age of one hundred and six as the story begins...

Chapter Twenty-Seven

Sooner than You Think

"What's a beautiful girl like you doing in a dive like this?" Stone slurred his words and leaned his arm on the bar beside the blonde with the crystal blue eyes.

The look she gave Monroe clearly shouted *help!* That was Monroe's cue to jump into action. He slid off his barstool and strode confidently over to her. He wrapped his arm around her shoulders protectively and nodded to the bartender, then focused his attention on his teammate. "Hey, Stone, I see you've met my date."

"Your date?" Stone took a step back. "I ain't seen you with her."

"We just met a few minutes ago," Monroe told his buddy. In reality, he and the woman had been flirting across the bar for about twenty minutes, and he was trying to work up the nerve to come introduce himself.

Just then, the bartender presented a beer for Monroe and whatever drink the blonde had been nursing. "Here you are, Monroe. And another for the lady."

"Thank you," the blonde said to Monroe, then asked, "is Stone a friend of yours, Monroe?"

"Yes, would you like to introduce yourself to him?" Monroe tried to communicate with his eyes that he couldn't exactly do that for her since he didn't know her name.

"I'm Bree." She held out her hand to Stone. "Any friend of Monroe's is a friend of mine."

Stone pulled Bree's hand to his lips for a kiss. "When yer ready to ditch lover-boy here, I can show you how good a friend I kin be."

Bree quickly pulled her hand away from Stone, wiped it on her jeans, and leaned closer to Monroe. "That would be rude to my date. But thank you for the offer."

"Hey, Stone." Their teammate, Blake, came up behind Stone and pulled him gently away from Bree and Monroe. "Why don't you challenge me to a game of pool? Raymond just isn't enough competition for me." Blake winked at Bree, rolled his eyes at Monroe, and led Stone over to the billiards table.

"Thank you," Bree mouthed at Blake, then turned to Monroe. "And thank *you*. Ugh, what is it with drunk guys hitting on ladies who just want to sit down with a drink at the end of a long day?"

"I don't know." Monroe unwrapped himself from Bree in case she thought he was one of those drunk guys who hit on ladies. "I've never been drunk before." Monroe took another pull from his bottle of beer and grinned at her.

"Yeah, right." Bree's playful eyes told Monroe she wouldn't mind if he hit on her, but he was determined to be a gentleman. There was a clicking and thumping as the balls on the billiard table dispersed in a clean break that probably put Blake at an advantage over Stone.

"Back to Stone's original question," Monroe said. "What *are* you doing in a dive like this?"

"I love Mexican food, and this looked like just the place to order some." The joint was a Mexican restaurant in food only. Country music flowed from the speakers rather than Mariachi music, glasses clinked behind the bar, guys cheered each other on while throwing darts, and ladies showed up with one thing on their minds—meeting an officer from Eglin Air Force Base.

"Have you ordered already?" Monroe asked, hoping to escort her to one of the booths and buy her dinner.

As if on cue, the bartender set a Styrofoam box in front of her, and she slipped him a twenty-dollar bill. "Keep the change."

"Taking your meal to go, huh?" Monroe tried to hide his disappointment. He grabbed a pen from the mug on the bar and wrote his cell phone number on the top of her Styrofoam box. "In case you need someone to talk to later while you're enjoying your meal."

Like a summons from Hades, Monroe felt the phone in his pocket vibrate and knew the text wasn't from Bree. In his peripheral vision, he watched as everyone on his team pulled out their cell phones with an identical text.

Monroe swore under his breath then looked up at Bree. "Duty calls."

"Looks that way." She smiled at him with feigned wistfulness.

"Sorry I won't be able to talk on the phone tonight, but maybe you could send me a text, and we could hang out when I get home from wherever it is the Army is sending me." Monroe tapped the number he'd written on her to-go box.

"Stay safe, Monroe." She pulled her cell phone from her purse. Good, maybe she *would* send him a text.

"I always do." Monroe leaned down and kissed her cheek, then lifted his focus and called out to his team. "Let's go, guys, wheels up in an hour."

"Comin', Cap'n," Stone slurred.

Blake called out to the bartender, "Can I get some coffee to go?" Blake pointed to Stone.

"Nice meeting you, Bree." Monroe patted her on the shoulder as he headed over to help Blake drag Stone from the bar. "See you soon."

"Maybe sooner than you think," she said.

Monroe wasn't sure what she meant by that but shook off her comment and balanced Stone between himself and Blake. The bartender handed Blake a Styrofoam cup of coffee, Davis fell in behind them, and Raymond held open the door. Time to get sobered up and hope wherever they were going was far enough away for Stone to get some sleep on the plane.

"Gonna be a long night," Monroe grumbled. "Time to catch some bad guys."

Chapter Twenty-Eight

Lieutenant Turner

"Gentlemen, I'd like to introduce our new intelligence analyst, Lieutenant Brianna Turner." The team's commander of operations, Judd Black, strode into the cargo bay of the transport aircraft followed by the most beautiful woman Monroe had ever seen.

She also happened to be the woman Monroe had hit on at the bar forty-five minutes prior. Bree, short for Brianna, short for Lieutenant Turner, short for the woman he could never hit on again for the rest of eternity. No two members of the same team could date, flirt with, sleep with, or marry. Relationships between team members were strictly forbidden.

Commander Black continued. "I would have liked to have more time to work together before heading out on a mission, but this is too important, and we can't wait." Even as he spoke, the cargo doors of the plane started closing.

Lieutenant Turner glanced around at the group of guys with her chin raised in confidence and a light smirk. Monroe saw that Bree knew in advance who was on her team, and she bit her lower lip. Was that humor? How long had she known? Probably the minute everyone's phones lit up while they were at the bar.

There were murmurs, chuckles, and snickers around the group when they all recognized her as well.

"Ain't that yer little chickee pie who you got naked with earlier tonight at the bar?" Stone stage-whispered to Monroe.

"I have *not* seen her naked," Monroe said, a little too loud. Conversations halted all around him, and he glared at Stone for implying that he had.

Commander Black, the man they all feared through a healthy dose of respect, lowered his clipboard and raised his eyebrows. "Thank you for clarifying that, Captain. Didn't realize you were dating anyone, but your personal life stays outside this airplane."

"I'm just sayin'," Stone said through his drunken stupor. "If you hadn't kissed her, we wouldn't be havin' this conversation."

"I didn't kiss her!" Monroe threw his hands in the air, exasperated.

"You kissed her, man, I saw you," Raymond said with a gleam in his eyes. *Traitor.*

"On the cheek." Monroe pointed to his own cheek, then glanced across the room at Bree. "That was before I knew who she was." His voice lowered with remorse, and he sighed.

"Is there a problem here, gentlemen," Commander Black asked. No one jumped up with an answer, and Monroe took it upon himself to explain.

"Sir, a few of us met Lieutenant Turner at the bar earlier this evening." Monroe took a breath and blew it out slowly. "Not realizing she was our new intelligence analyst, a couple of the guys... hit on her." He mumbled the last few words.

Commander Black turned around to look at Bree with his eyebrows raised. "Will this be uncomfortable for you, Lieutenant Turner?"

"Not at all, sir," Bree glanced at Monroe then back at their boss. "For the most part, they were gentlemen. And they didn't know who I was any more than I knew who they were. I have faith that we can all be adults and nothing will jeopardize our mission."

Monroe's shoulders softened, and he fought every primal urge not to wink at her in response to her declaration. She was so beyond off-limits they could both lose their jobs if they so much as looked at each other wrong.

"And none of you have seen each other naked?" the commander asked.

"No!" Bree and Monroe insisted at the same time. Monroe pinched the bridge of his nose and closed his eyes. This was going to be harder than he thought, and they'd only known each other for an hour.

Stone stepped closer and wrapped his arm around Monroe's shoulders. "I see Cap'n naked almost every day in the shower."

Monroe shrugged out from under Stone's arm and pushed him away. "You drunk idiot. Go sleep it off somewhere. We're jumping out of this airplane in six hours whether you've sobered up or not, so I'd suggest you sober up."

"I'd suggest we have a listen to whatever Commander Black has to tell us about this here mission," Stone said, sounding more sober than he probably was. "Then I will find a hammock and sleep until y'all strap a parachute on my back and toss me out the back of this here air-o-plane."

"Thank you for permission, Lieutenant Stone." Commander Black's sarcasm hung in the air.

"Yer welcome, Commander." Stone swayed a little as if they were already in the air and had encountered some turbulence.

"A captain from the 20th Special Forces Group is stuck behind enemy lines along with a small group of volunteer soldiers from a local Mayan tribe near El Pilar along the disputed border between Guatemala and Belize," Commander Black said. "Tensions are high, and a rescue team would have to drive through Belize and past enemy combatants in order to reach our stranded brothers. We're going to drop in on them and get those boys out."

"What are our guys doing in Belize?" Monroe asked, folding his arms across his chest. The minute he asked the question, he knew exactly who was with the Mayan kids and his heart sunk. How could Henry be this stupid?

Bree interjected. "The local Mayan tribe has been terrorized by insurgents who have been stealing their women and children to sell them as sex slaves."

"The boys from the 20th SFG are trying to break up a human trafficking ring?" Raymond asked.

"How did these guys even get on the radar?" Blake asked. "The National Guard doesn't usually get involved in operations in Belize."

"One of the Sayid princes went down there to meet up with a girlfriend, and she told them about the tribe and the human trafficking," Bree said.

"Those pretty boy princes who abandoned their country to become playboys in America?" Blake asked.

Monroe's stomach plummeted. None of his team knew about his affiliation with the Sayids. He had a feeling they were all about to find out.

Bree continued as if Blake hadn't interrupted. "That prince has an uncle in the United States Senate and pulled some strings to get the U.S. involved."

"Senator Alejandro Cohen is their grandfather actually." Monroe spoke loud enough that most people in the room turned to him.

"Cohen? Any relation to you, Captain?" Commander Black asked.

"Senator Cohen is my grandfather as well," Monroe said. "The Sayid princes... are my cousins."

Chapter Twenty-Nine

Briefing

"This whole situation doesn't really surprise me," Monroe said, still dumbfounded and disappointed that the gorgeous girl he met at the bar was actually Lieutenant Brianna Turner, Alpha Team's new intelligence analyst. He was also incredulous that his cousin, Henry, could be stupid enough to lead a group of teenagers into a situation so dangerous the Special Forces airborne unit needed to rescue them. "We just talked about the kidnapped girls at Prince Augustus's wedding last week."

"You attended a Sayid royal wedding?" Blake asked, awe in his voice.

"Spoken by a man who a moment ago referred to them as playboy princes who abandoned their country?"

"Yeah, well, royalty is royalty." Blake shrugged. As young as he was, Blake probably would have been just as impressed to meet a movie star. The little rookie was probably closer in age to the princes than to most of the team.

"The grass isn't always greener on the other side of the castle moat," Monroe said. "My spoiled little cousins have learned some life lessons the hard way. But that's not why we're dropping into a hornets' nest to rescue some freedom warriors fighting a human trafficking ring."

"How did you know about the freedom warriors?" Bree crossed her arms and narrowed her eyes. "We hadn't divulged that information."

"I told you we just talked about this last week. Prince Aaron and his wife, Felicia were trying to get the senator to help, and I suggested they talk to our cousin, Army Captain Henry Stephenson because he's knowledgeable about refugees. He told Aaron he could get them in touch with the guys from Operation Freedom Warriors."

"Another cousin?" Raymond asked. As Monroe's second in command, Raymond probably knew more about Monroe than all the other guys on the team combined. But Monroe had never divulged his connection with his grandfather, Senator Cohen, or with the Sayid princes.

"I thought Prince Augustus got married, not Prince Aaron. I'm confused." Stone scratched his head. As drunk as he still was, Monroe wasn't surprised he was confused.

Commander Judd Black glared at Monroe from where he stood with his clipboard. "You encouraged Captain Stephenson to lead a team of vigilantes on a twelve-hour hike to rescue refugees from human traffickers in a foreign country without direct orders?"

"I didn't encourage him to disobey orders. I just encouraged him to talk to Aaron and Felicia." Monroe glanced at Stone. "Who, by the way, got married the day before Augustus and Phoebe."

"I think I need a nap," Stone said.

Davis, their logistics expert, piped in. "Let's finish our briefing first, and then you can find your blankie and footie pajamas and tuck yourself in for a nice long airplane ride." He loved to razz Stone about his tendency to fall asleep whenever they started into a mission.

The reality was, Stone was rarely sober enough to be on a mission. But he was the best weapons expert Monroe had ever seen, and technically Stone wasn't on duty. Unless an emergency popped up, like today. In which case, they were all on duty. Drop everything and get on the plane. Wheels up and strap on your chute. No questions.

Today, the fight was personal. Monroe needed to get his head straight. His cousin was in trouble. He looked up at Bree. "Lieutenant Turner, we apologize for the interruption. Could you continue explaining the situation in Belize?"

"Thank you, Captain." Bree nodded, a mask of professionalism hiding an underlying tension that would probably exist between them for a long time. "As Commander Black mentioned, Captain Stephenson organized a group of teenagers into a makeshift company and led them into battle without prior authorization and is now caught behind enemy lines with nothing but a crumbling citadel as a stronghold. They'll be lucky if they make it until morning."

Monroe cringed, thinking about any soldier in harm's way, in particular a family member.

Commander Black interjected again. "This operation toes the line between politics and our military strategy in the region."

"Which is what, exactly?" Raymond crossed his arms and creased his brow.

"Security, governance, economics, protecting American citizens abroad and avoiding transnational crime," Commander Black said.

"Well, if that ain't the vaguest military strategy I ever heard," Stone said.

"That's the mission. You don't have to like it. You just need to get those boys out."

"What about the kidnapped girls?" Monroe asked. "Did they get safely out?"

"Ten of them did," Bree said. "They have a twelve hour walk back to the reservation. We may get there before they do, which means we'll probably offer some assistance to them as well. But those boys need immediate extraction, and they're running low on ammunition."

"Now, here's the kicker." Commander Black glanced around. "The kidnappers need to be alive and coherent in order to track down the remaining traffickers and find the other missing girls."

There were moans and groans around the cargo bay as the rangers found their seats and strapped themselves in. The plane taxied down the runway and Monroe grumbled under his breath an indiscriminate string of curse words. Taking prisoners was different than eliminating the threat. This mission just got a heck of a lot worse.

Chapter Thirty

Good Luck with That

"Could I have a word with you, Lieutenant Turner?" Monroe asked. The butterflies in his stomach had nothing to do with turbulence nor the two beers he drank at the bar earlier. He hadn't waited thirty seconds past the all-clear to move about the cargo bay before unclipping from his seat and approaching Bree. Now standing before her, he wondered if he'd made a mistake.

Bree's light brown hair, which had rested on her shoulders in waves when they'd met at the bar, was tucked up in neat braids that wrapped around either side of her head. Her crystal blue eyes blinked up at Monroe with purposeful innocence. "Of course, Captain. How can I help you?"

Oh, what a loaded question that was. If he told her the answer that was niggling at the back of his mind, she'd either slap him or insist he be moved to a different team. That was a risk he wouldn't take. "I just wanted to apologize for hitting on you earlier."

"There's nothing to apologize for, Captain." Bree's confidence seemed forced. "Don't worry about it. You didn't know who I was any more than I knew who you were. Plus, I was flirting right back. This is just as much my doing as it was yours."

"I just don't want things to get awkward between the two of us." Monroe searched Bree's eyes and saw regret and disappointment. Maybe she had been just as excited to call him as he had been to receive a call from her.

"I can't imagine things getting any more awkward than Stone asking if you'd seen me naked."

Monroe laughed out loud, drawing the attention of several of his teammates. Oops. "Thank goodness I hadn't or you and I could have been separated before we had a chance to get to know each other."

"We're not really supposed to be getting to know each other, right?" Bree raised her eyebrows.

"I've never had a problem getting to know any of the other handlers who serve our team."

"Did you flirt with any of the other handlers?" she asked pointedly. "Did you give your phone number to any of the other handlers?"

"No, ma'am, I did not." Monroe scuffed his foot against the floor of the C-130 Hercules transport plane.

"Let's just call a truce and agree to go forward from here." Bree reached her hand out. "As friends."

"As friends," Monroe agreed, returning her handshake. When she placed her hand in his, electricity flowed between them. "Oh, this is going to be way harder than I thought it would be."

"Way harder," she said, her eyes smoldering.

"I'm going to walk to the other end of the cargo hold and mentally prepare myself for this jump and this mission." Monroe gripped her hand just a little tighter. "And I'm going to try to forget you are on this airplane."

"Good luck with that, Captain." Bree's voice was soft and filled with regret.

"Thanks, I'm going to need it." Monroe released her hand and descended the metal stairs to where the rest of his teammates were hanging hammocks and taking inventory of supplies. He ignored the multiple sets of eyes that followed him to where he usually hung his hammock. True to his word, Monroe grabbed his pack and kept walking all the way to the back.

Not surprisingly, Raymond followed and set his pack beside Monroe's. Without any commentary, they hung their hammocks beside each other and climbed in.

Monroe pulled his ball cap down over his face to block out the light and to try to forget the beautiful vixen who would haunt his dreams from the other end of the plane.

"Wanna talk about it?" Ray asked.

"Nope."

"Let me know if you change your mind."

"There's nothing to talk about, Lieutenant." Monroe didn't mean to sound terse, and he softened his tone. "Off limits. End of discussion."

Ray snorted with barely restrained laughter. "Good luck with that."

"That's what she said too..."

Chapter Thirty-One

ISR Reports Show

Never again. When the message was passed down the line of jumpers that it was time to wake up, Monroe wasn't the first to receive the orders. Normally he would have hung his hammock closest to the front of the cargo bay and heard the orders directly from Commander Black.

Even a woman as intriguing as Lieutenant Brianna Turner wasn't worth losing his job over or risking the safety of his mission. Hanging his hammock at the far end of the transport plane just to avoid being close to her meant that he was literally the last to know they were close to their destination.

None of the guys had really fallen asleep while resting, other than Stone, who snored when they tried to wake him, rolled over, and crashed to the floor.

"Well, that's one way to wake up," Monroe grumbled, stepping around his teammate. The guys should have cut him off earlier while back at the bar. Not that anyone could have predicted they'd be flying out on a mission that night, but the team needed to stay better prepared.

Monroe strode with purpose to the cooler and pulled out a bottle of Powerade. He gulped down half the bottle, tasting the salty electrolytes as they restored his body from a slight hangover. He'd had too much to drink as well.

As Monroe capped the beverage, he caught Bree's gaze from a few feet away. He nodded to her. "Good morning, Lieutenant."

"Good morning, Captain," she replied without emotion.

Monroe wasn't sure which was worse—awkward awareness of their attraction or cold and unfeeling indifference.

One by one, the guys followed his lead and reached into the cooler. Then they all stood around, waiting for further instructions.

"Okay, guys, listen up." Commander Black stepped in front of them. "We're almost to the jump zone, and I want to share with you some up-to-date intel. ISR shows a campsite with four tents, six men, all armed and all injured. To the south end of the site there's a crumbling citadel where Captain Stephenson's team is presumed to be keeping a stronghold. All eighteen heat signatures are bright, so we're assuming they're alive and kicking. That's a good sign."

"What's not a good sign"—Bree took over and continued the explanation—"is that the campsite appears to be the only drop zone for miles around, which means you're landing hot and can anticipate taking fire immediately. In retaliation, aim for the legs and try not to kill anyone."

"Can we see this surveillance data?" Monroe asked. "If we can't get close enough to conduct on-the-ground reconnaissance, we have to be able to trust intel from the sky. I want to see what we're jumping into."

"We will have up-to-date ISR in about five minutes," Bree said. "We'll also have a UAV in the air, and I'll have control of the drone myself."

"While that's reassuring, Lieutenant, can you explain why these guys are so important to be kept alive?" Monroe knew it was imperative that his team understood the importance of this mission. They were putting their lives on the line. They needed to know why.

"Twenty-four teenage girls were kidnapped from the Mayan reservation," Bree explained. "Only ten girls have been recovered. Young girls are too valuable for the kidnappers to have killed, especially if they're virgins, which means they've already been trafficked elsewhere. We need to know where. The only way we're going to learn the whereabouts of those girls is if we can interrogate the kidnappers. When you're considering where to aim your shotgun, you picture those young girls' faces... and aim for his kneecaps."

"I can think of a location that would hurt worse than the kneecaps," Stone grumbled.

"That would definitely send a message," Raymond said with a sneer.

Monroe lowered his gaze and fought a bout of nausea, wishing he could blame the hangover or the pitch of the airplane. Picturing young girls being sold as sex slaves was repulsive. Anger replaced the nausea, and he grumbled a menacing command. "Get me in the air. These guys are going down."

"Gentlemen, strap on your packs and get ready for some fireworks," Commander Black said. "We'll download the final ISR data from the satellite and show you the intelligence before you jump."

Without further orders, the guys dispersed to their gear and strapped on their parachutes, scowls on their faces. Having Lieutenant Turner explain the gravity of the situation was just what the team needed to be motivated enough to complete this mission without hesitation.

Chapter Thirty-Two

Fight Ain't Over Yet

T he intelligence, surveillance, and reconnaissance data from the ISR satellite was spot-on. By the time Monroe's parachute opened, he felt as if he'd been given a personal tour of the kidnappers' campsite.

Although they appeared injured and tired from having been awake through the night, the kidnappers were armed and on high alert. The sun had crested the horizon, and the kidnappers had a clear view of the citadel. Yet they didn't seem to be on the offensive. More they were waiting for Henry and his team of amateur vigilantes to emerge from their stronghold. That or they were waiting for backup.

Whatever the kidnappers were doing, they weren't expecting five air-borne rangers from the United States Army to drop out of the sky.

Which meant Monroe and his team didn't take fire until they were almost on the ground.

Without waiting to unhook their parachutes, all five rangers shot first, planning to ask questions later. All six kidnappers were on the ground, writhing in pain before Monroe took a single step into the campsite.

He should have known rescuing Henry and his boys wouldn't be that easy.

Bree's voice came through his com. "Be advised you have three unknown vehicles rapidly approaching your position from the south."

"Copy that." Monroe glanced to the road where a Jeep with mud on its deflated tires blocked access from that direction. Good, the insurgents would have to leave their vehicles in order to fight.

Monroe was going to assume that the approaching insurgents were as unprepared as the kidnappers. They wouldn't be expecting an airborne Special Forces unit for a welcome party.

"Get those guys tied up before their buddies arrive. I'm going to check on Captain Stephenson and his boys." Monroe ran hard to the west side of the clearing, calling out when he got within range of fire. "United States Army! Do not shoot!" He repeated his call in Spanish.

"Monroe!" Henry's startled face showed over the barrier and then disappeared again.

As Monroe entered the citadel and hurried up the stairs, he understood why the kidnappers hadn't pursued Henry's squad when they took shelter in this crumbling stronghold. The men wouldn't have made it up the first flight of stairs without being shot from above. Anyone entering this maze of switchback staircases was a sitting duck.

If Henry wanted Monroe dead right now, he would already be falling. This structure was the only reason these boys were still alive. They'd managed to hold their position, but they were surrounded on all sides.

When he reached the top of the stairs, Monroe took inventory. They were a bunch of little boys. The oldest couldn't have been more than eighteen or nineteen. They were ragged, filthy, and exhausted. Monroe turned to his cousin and shoved him hard.

"What were you thinking?" When Monroe pushed Henry, he barely faltered before shoving right back.

"I was thinking about twenty-four girls who needed our help!" Henry shouted in defense.

"These are just kids, Henry! You idiot!"

All seventeen teenagers stood and raised their chins confidently.

"These boys have fought more valiantly than any soldiers I've ever led," Henry said with pride in his voice.

"They're unprotected! They have no armor. They're fighting with hunting rifles and crossbows. They could have been killed... *you* could have been killed." Monroe halted his impassioned rant and pulled Henry into his arms. Just short of allowing his emotions to crack his facade, Monroe gripped his cousin fiercely. "You could have been killed."

"Thank you for rescuing us." Henry returned the hug with an equal amount of emotion in his tired voice.

"Fight ain't over yet." Monroe pulled away. "We have insurgents approaching from the south. You need to stay right here until we eliminate the threat."

"I want to help." An older boy in the group stepped forward and spoke in Spanish.

"Me too," another kid said. Other boys nodded in agreement.

"No." Monroe insisted. "You're wearing T-shirts, not bulletproof vests. Don't act brave. Nothing good will come from you getting yourselves killed."

Monroe pressed his com to speak directly to Bree. "Lieutenant, what's the ETA on the approaching vehicles?"

"Three clicks out," Bree said. "The Belizean government has been made aware of your situation, and they're sending help."

"Any idea how many insurgents are in those vehicles?"

"No, Captain, but they seem to be large enough to fit about five men each so assume no more than fifteen. You also have two Pave Hawks inbound to extract your boys and assist with detaining the insurgents."

"Copy that, Lieutenant." Monroe turned to Henry to relay the news. "We've got two helicopters inbound to give you a lift home. Plus, the Belizean government is sending in reinforcements."

"They won't help," the oldest boy said with sarcasm and disdain. "They haven't helped yet. What makes you think they'll help now?"

"Because nobody messes with the boys from the U.S. of A." Monroe lifted a fist and Henry bumped knuckles. "Trust me. They don't want us here. And they don't want the wrath of our military presence."

"Captain," Bree's voice entered his com. "Your friends have arrived."

Chapter Thirty-Three

Strategic Entrance

"I'm serious. You kids stay here." Monroe pointed to each of the guys who had stepped forward, commanding with his eyes and his stern tone. Then he turned to Henry. "You too. Unless you have a suit of Kevlar hiding underneath that Army T-shirt and a Beretta 9mm clipped to your belt, stay in this citadel. You got it? I can't fight these guys and worry that I'm gonna have to look your momma in the eye and tell her you tried to play hero and paid the ultimate price. Are we clear?"

"Crystal clear," Henry grumbled through clenched teeth.

"Captain, get down here!" Raymond's voice rang through Monroe's com. "We're taking heavy fire."

"I'm on my way," Monroe said to Raymond, then turned to Henry and the boys and commanded one more time. "You stay here!"

Monroe hurried back down the switchback stairs but hesitated at the bottom. Before peeking around the corner, he asked Bree through his com to give him up-to-date intel from her drone.

"Lieutenant Turner, this is Alpha One, give me an idea where everybody is."

"I have eyes on six insurgents near the Jeep," Bree said. "Alpha team is near the tents. All kidnappers are tied up behind the tents, and the insurgents don't seem to know where their friends are."

"Good, let's keep it that way," Monroe said. "How heavily armed are the six?"

"I don't see any firepower greater than the semi-automatic rifles they have in their hands," Bree said. "I don't think you're dealing with paramilitary insurgents. But you are dealing with professionals. And they weren't expecting you. I think these guys would have been transporting the girls to the new location. We need to keep them alive."

"Copy that, Lieutenant." *Now what?* Monroe peeked around the corner of the entrance to the citadel and took inventory of his surroundings. All four of his guys hid behind the tents, which offered very little protection, and shot at the insurgents near the Jeep.

Monroe had the advantage that the insurgents had no idea he even existed. He skirted along the edge of the campsite to where a long, narrow rock structure traversed the length of the campsite. The ancient row of stones could have been a building foundation or a fencerow. Today the stones acted as a fortress.

Having trained as a sharpshooter, Monroe took out several insurgents by tagging them in their right shoulders and knocking their guns out of their hands. Almost instantly the other insurgents turned on him, giving Alpha team the opportunity to fire without returning shots. Several more guys went down.

His team members were successfully hitting the arms and the legs of the insurgents, keeping most of the men alive but incapacitated. Several of them were probably dead, unfortunately, but Monroe had little remorse for taking the life of men who were raping and selling little girls.

Hiding behind the rock structure, Monroe crawled closer to the insurgents and shot again, hitting his mark with ease. They were down to two insurgents who were using the Jeep as cover. There was no way to get to them without exposing himself beyond the rock wall. They were at an impasse.

From the other side of the campsite, four hunting rifles went off in quick succession, and the remaining two insurgents fell.

Just like that, a deafening quiet resounded through the campsite. A man Monroe had never met before stood with three teenagers near the entrance to what appeared to be a trail leading into the woods. Whoever they were, they'd saved Alpha team. All four of them crept forward, rifles aimed at the insurgents in case any of them so much as moved a hand toward their gun. Monroe and the rest of Alpha team also crept forward, guns trained on the insurgents.

When they advanced from three sides to a point in which they were almost aiming at each other, Monroe called out, "Halt." All three groups stopped but kept their guns on the insurgents.

Monroe met the gaze of the team leader of the four and called out, "Stand down." Then to his teammates, he said, "Alpha team, advance and take these men into custody."

The man and his three teenagers, so similar to the group of teens hiding with Henry, raised their rifles to the sky but remained on high alert.

Alpha team crept forward one foot at a time.

One of the insurgents reached for his gun and Monroe pulled his trigger instinctively. Oops. Killed another one. Hopefully the remaining insurgents would provide the needed intelligence to find the missing girls.

Within a few minutes, all living insurgents were tied up with zip ties, and all deceased insurgents were catalogued. There were a total of five dead and eleven in custody.

Henry emerged from the citadel with his seventeen teenagers. Prior to any introductions, Monroe heard Henry compliment the guy who'd emerged from the woods with hunting rifles. "Nice shooting, Xavier."

"Thanks, man. Glad you're all safe," Xavier said.

"Way to use your entrance strategically," Monroe said to Xavier. "Well done."

"Twelve years in Homeland Security and five in the CIA finally paid off," Xavier joked, and they all chuckled with subdued humor. There was nothing funny about the situation, and they still had a great deal of work ahead of them to find the missing girls. But the immediate threat had been eliminated, and a reprieve was greatly appreciated.

Bree's soothing voice rang into Monroe's ear. "Alpha One, be advised you have two Pave Hawks inbound to extract your boys and assist with detaining the insurgents."

"Copy that, Lieutenant," Monroe said. Then in a more subdued voice he broke from his formal cadence and spoke directly to the woman behind the com. "And, Bree, thanks for being our eyes this morning. We couldn't have done this without you."

Chapter Thirty-Four

You Will Do as You're Told

"What do you mean they're taking the kidnappers into custody?" Monroe turned on Commander Black with anger in his words. After the teenagers had all been airlifted back to the reservation, Alpha team worked together with Xavier, Henry, and two police officers who had been sent by the Belizean government to formally arrest the kidnappers.

"Captain, we are not sanctioned to be here," Commander Black responded. "These men are on Belizean soil, and we have no jurisdiction." When they were flown from the kidnappers' campsite to the Mayan reservation, Monroe had no idea the insurgents would be transported somewhere else.

"We won't even have a chance to interrogate them? How are we supposed to find the human trafficking ring? Are we back to square one?" Monroe was baffled by what he was hearing.

"We're not back to square one. We have rescued Captain Stephenson and seventeen teenage boys who were trapped behind enemy lines." As if to prove his point, Commander Black and Monroe both glanced to the other end of the community center that was acting as their makeshift base of operations. A triage station had been prepared to help clean up the injuries.

Henry met Monroe's gaze from across the room and lifted his chin in acknowledgement. No one had addressed the issue of Henry's insubordination in leading a group of untrained teenagers on a twelve-hour trek. Every single one of those boys had been injured. Henry would probably be court-marshalled and demoted. Monroe instinctively knew he would have done the same thing if he'd been in Henry's shoes.

"But we don't know where the remaining fourteen girls are." Monroe brought his attention back to his commanding officer.

"No, we don't." Commander Black folded his arms across his chest.

"Then how are we going to find those girls?" Monroe's confidence was waning.

"We're going to allow the Belizean government to take the lead and do the interrogations."

"What kind of interrogations though? Are we talking enhanced interrogation? Or are they just going to sit the guys down, feed them breakfast, and ask nicely if they'll tell them the location of the human trafficking ring? The Belizean police officers aren't going to find out where the girls are using those tactics."

"We don't know that," Commander Black said. "They may have interrogation methods that we aren't aware of and might be able to get the information needed from the kidnappers."

"I wanna talk to these guys myself," Monroe insisted. "I didn't come all this way to go back home without having saved those girls."

"Captain, you were not asked to save those girls. You were asked to rescue Captain Stephenson and those seventeen boys who were trapped. We did our job. We got those boys out, and that's all that matters. It's time we head home to the States."

"I am not leaving Belize without rescuing those girls!" Monroe gripped his hands into fists.

"Captain, you will go where you're told." How could Commander Black be so calm and cold? This was serious. "You are not in charge of this mission."

"No, I'm only in charge when the bullets are flying." Monroe shook his head with disdain. "I wanna see the brass making these decisions stand out on that field and take down the insurgents and see the fear on the faces of those young soldiers putting their life on the line. They need to think of the terror in those little girls' eyes and then decide who stays, who goes, and who conducts the interrogations."

Monroe pushed past his commanding officer and stormed out of the community center. Without meeting the gazes of any other of his teammates, he marched up the hill toward the parking lot of the El Pilar archaeological site, needing to be alone with his anger.

Chapter Thirty-Five

In Another Lifetime

S oft footfalls crunched against the gravel on the path behind him, and Monroe hoped the person approaching was not Bree. Or maybe he hoped it was Bree. The empty parking lot at the El Pilar archeological site was the perfect spot for him to pace and fume as he calmed himself down after his argument with Commander Black.

Monroe turned around and stood face-to-face with the beautiful woman who had been communicating with him all morning. Monroe could hardly believe they had met for the first time less than twenty-four hours ago. With all that had happened in the past day, it seemed as if they'd known each other for years. Having her voice in his com the whole time he was executing the op had been intoxicating.

He understood now why people on the same team shouldn't date or fall in love. The risk was too strong that they would put their emotions ahead of the mission and do something that might compromise the op. It was hard enough having loved ones somewhere in the world who would miss him if he were gone. It was different altogether to have someone right there close giving him directions and orders and have them give those orders in the spirit of protecting him rather than completing the op. The mission could be jeopardized because of their bias and unwillingness to send the other into danger.

"You shouldn't be up here." Even as Monroe said the words, he recognized how badly he wanted her to be up here.

"I was worried about you." She folded her arms across her chest as if forcing herself not to reach out to him.

"Well, don't be." Monroe turned around with a huff.

"Do you want to talk about what happened?"

"Nope." He knew what she meant. When he'd finished the op and allowed his emotions to soften his tone and speak to her directly, he'd crossed a line. So far no one else had called him on it, but Monroe was positive he'd get a slap on the wrist eventually.

"We have to address this attraction eventually you know." Bree's voice was soft, understanding.

"We don't need to address anything. You are off limits. Period. End of story."

"I have a hard time believing that this is the end of our story," Bree said. "We feel too much of a connection to one another to walk away now."

"I care about you enough to walk away." Was he lying to himself? How could he care about someone he'd known for a few hours? All he was feeling was gratitude for her help that morning, and attraction misdirected by her beauty and compassion.

"Well, I care about you enough to force you to stay." She stepped forward and wrapped her arms around his waist, pulling him close.

Monroe reluctantly returned her embrace with a groan. As he held her in his arms, he drank in the scent of her hair, memorizing the fragrance of her skin. He pressed his lips to her forehead.

"We can't do this, Bree. As much as I desperately want you right now, I won't risk your job or your future to satisfy one moment of weakness. No matter how tempting you are."

"Job or no job, I can't risk throwing away the feelings I have when looking into your eyes," she said. "Or hearing your voice." That was more accurate.

"Brianna," Monroe whispered. That was the first time he called her Brianna. He usually addressed her as Lieutenant Turner or Bree. But she was more than a Bree. She was a Brianna. "I've never felt this way before."

"Me neither." Brianna squeezed a little tighter, but he knew this had to stop here and now. She felt so good in his arms, he didn't want to let her go.

"Maybe in another lifetime I could've been with you," he said. "But there's just no way." Monroe kissed her forehead one more time, released her from his arms, and walked back down the path.

Chapter Thirty-Six

Get Me a Live Microphone

"**Y**ou need to calm down, Captain," Raymond said. "This isn't something you have any control over, so you need to put it from your mind." Ray was right, but Monroe wasn't ready to let this go. He was still fuming about not having the opportunity to interrogate the insurgents.

Monroe grunted at his second in command and best friend, not wanting to admit the other reason he still had a scowl on his face. In an attempt to escape the temptation of spending more time alone with Lieutenant Brianna Turner, Monroe had strode back into the community center that they were using as a makeshift command center on the Mayan reservation. The room was fuller than when he stormed out twenty minutes prior.

Prince Aaron Sayid and his bride, Felicia, had joined their cousin, Captain Henry Stephenson. Monroe bypassed his teammates in favor of reuniting with family.

"Hey, man, good to see you." Monroe embraced Aaron and then lifted Felicia into a hug. She was so adorably petite and youthful it was hard to believe she was twenty-one years old. Both she and Aaron were two years younger than Monroe and Henry, yet they felt decades apart in maturity.

There was something special about dedicating one's life to service in the military that allowed Monroe and Henry to grow up faster than their spoiled cousin. A year ago, both of them would have looked down their noses at Aaron because of his irresponsibility and playboy attitude. Even now Monroe wasn't sure how much Aaron had really changed.

There was a commotion outside, and all heads turned toward the door when the oldest teenage boy who had been hiding with Henry came to the door and called out, "The girls are back!"

At first Monroe thought the young man meant the missing fourteen girls had returned. But in reality, he meant the ten girls who Henry's team had rescued from the kidnappers. The girls and the amateur platoon of teenage boys had finally finished their twelve-hour trek and entered the reservation exhausted and filthy.

Henry unexpectedly pushed past Monroe and out the door. Monroe glanced at Aaron and raised his eyebrows.

"He probably wants to see that cute little humanitarian aid worker he was so enthralled with," Aaron said.

"That would explain his urgency if there was a woman involved," Monroe said. "Come on, let's go meet her."

"We've met Whitney," Felicia said, leading the way. "She's the woman who helps the girls when they get rescued."

"She's in charge of the aftercare program for Operation Freedom Warriors," Aaron said. "She's really nice."

Monroe followed his cousins to go meet Whitney.

The courtyard outside the community center was bustling with tears of relief as parents were reunited with their kidnapped daughters.

Henry stood in the middle of all the commotion, holding a beautiful but fatigued young woman who clung to him, nearly collapsed in his arms. He was talking softly to her and smoothing her hair almost as if he were petting an exhausted and beloved Golden Retriever.

Love. That was the emotion emanating from Henry and Whitney. How they could have fallen in love so quickly when they'd known each other for only a few days was beyond Monroe's understanding. But there was no other way to explain the tender way Henry was holding Whitney.

Monroe's gaze was drawn from the reunited couple to where Brianna stood across the courtyard. He looked away quickly in case someone caught the undeniable electricity that sparked between them.

He allowed his eyes to roam the crowd, watching the reunions but also seeing the disappointed looks in the eyes of the families whose girls were still missing. That angered him. There had to be more he could do for these people.

A plan started to form in Monroe's mind. It was risky. He would probably lose his job. Or be arrested. Or both. At least he'd be safe in the brig. The missing fourteen girls were living a nightmare today. Monroe couldn't think of his own comfort. He strode purposely back to his cousin.

"Your Highness, how easily can you pull together a press conference?" Monroe asked Aaron.

"Snap of my fingers," Aaron said, lifting his chin.

"Get me in front of a live microphone," Monroe grumbled.

"On it," Aaron said, already with his phone to his ear.

Chapter Thirty-Seven

You'll Both Lose Your Jobs

One phone call. That's all it took for Prince Aaron Sayid of Madain Saleh to convince a reporter from Channel 7 News out of Belize City to send a reporter. One was stationed in San Ignacio and hopped in a news van to drive up the mountain to El Pilar. Within forty-five minutes, a reporter was standing with a microphone in front of the prince and his two cousins.

There had been a tense moment when Henry refused to cooperate. They had insisted, but he wouldn't back down.

"Dude, I could lose my job!" Henry grumbled. "Don't ask me to stand beside you at that microphone."

"You're going to lose your job anyway," Monroe said. "You dragged a team of untrained teenage soldiers into a war zone without permission from your superiors. You are the reason that we're down here. Now come stand beside your cousins."

"No, *you* are the reason I'm down here because you suggested that I talk to Aaron and Felicia. I was happily dancing at a wedding when you dragged me into this."

"I didn't drag you into this," Monroe said. "Aaron dragged you into this. And you are the one who chose to lead those young boys into battle when you got down here."

"None of us are at fault," Aaron interrupted. "The kidnappers dragged us into this. When people are kidnapping little girls, this is an international problem. This is not a problem between cousins or Mayans or Belizeans or Guatemalans or Americans. This is an international problem, and it needs to be fixed. We need to stop arguing among ourselves and stand united in front of that microphone. You will likely *both* lose your jobs, but this is what needs to be done."

They all took a deep breath, calming themselves down.

Remorse clouded Henry's expression. "You're right of course," Henry said. "Let's do this."

They returned to stand before the reporter, confirmed they had a live feed, and stood together, Monroe as spokesperson.

"I've called this press conference and speak to the prime minister of Belize and all the democratically elected government officials. But I encourage the international community to hear what the government of Belize is doing... or *not* doing."

Although he knew this would get him into trouble with his commanding officers, Monroe couldn't see any other way than to expose the corruption in the Belizean government.

"You promised to protect the Mayans, who you forced into a treaty," Monroe continued. "If they would peacefully stay on their reservation and not fight, you would protect them."

Monroe wasn't sure how true that statement was, but he said it anyway. Yes, the Belizean government had promised not to fight the Mayans or kick them off their land. But they never really promised to protect the Mayans. More like tolerate them.

"You have been made aware that human traffickers are kidnapping the women and children of the peaceful Mayan people, and you are doing nothing to stop them. They pass right through your capital city, and you sit there and turn a blind eye. Your corruption is shameful. Your people are suffering."

His impassioned words rose in volume as he grew angrier.

"I want to know why you think it's okay to neglect the people you swore to protect," Monroe said. "This is modern day slavery. These women and children are being sold as sex slaves. They are being used to create child pornography. How can you sit back and allow this to happen?"

Monroe pointed to the west in the general direction of the contested border.

"And I blame the Guatemalan government as well. If you all hadn't been fighting over this border dispute for years, you could have come together and helped these people."

Again, he wasn't sure helping the people had ever been the intention, but it sounded logical, so he continued.

"How could any of you in the government be so corrupt that you allow the murdering and abducting of your people to take place unless you are in on it?" There, he'd said it. No going back. "What are you gaining from this? Money? Power? Are you raping these children also? Are you pedophiles too? Is that why you're turning a blind eye?"

The cameraman glared at Monroe from behind his camera, and the reporter's brow creased. Monroe was a foreigner on their soil accusing their government of wrongdoing. He considered toning down his message but knew they needed to hear this also.

"Maybe it's because your own women and children are not being abducted. If your wives and children were being enslaved would you turn a blind eye?"

He paused to let them consider his question.

"I call upon the international community and the UN Security Council to bring down the full force of international laws against the Belizean government and the Guatemalan government, unless you stop this corruption and this human trafficking that is happening right before your eyes and protect your people."

Monroe knew he was crossing a line. What did he want? War? Sanctions? Lines drawn in the sand? He decided to appeal to their humanity.

"If any of you in the Belizean government or the Guatemalan government still desires freedom for your people, stand up to this corruption, take back your government, stop this blatant violation of international laws and morality."

With one last menacing statement, Monroe drew his own line in the sand.

"This is your final warning. If I can't get the international community to help, I'll come there myself. I'm not afraid of you." Monroe turned on his heel and walked away from the makeshift press conference.

Chapter Thirty-Eight

Get Out of My Way

"What were you thinking?" Commander Judd Black bellowed close to Monroe's face. "You have no authority to address the international community like that or call out the Belizean government for corruption. You are not speaking on behalf of the United States government. You are a mere captain in the United States Army."

"I had to do something," Monroe yelled back, balling his fists at his sides. "We can't stand around and let this happen." Even standing here in a makeshift base of operations at the tribe's community center left him feeling helpless. He wanted to get out and find those missing girls.

"Then you report it to your superiors." The commander pointed in the direction of the parking lot up the hill. "You don't stand in front of a microphone and appeal to the United Nations Human Rights Coalition as if you represent the U.S. government."

They'd drawn a crowd near the community center. The families and teenagers were in awe of Monroe's bravery but most everyone else was dumbfounded at Monroe's stupidity in taking a stand.

"Well, nobody's doing anything about human trafficking," Monroe said, more calmly. The more he'd talked to Xavier and Henry that morning the angrier he'd become. And Prince Aaron's driver, Joab, had regaled him with stories of corruption at all levels of the Belizean government, including the prime minister's cabinet. "If I report the corruption to my superiors and they don't do anything about it, and they report it to their superiors, and they don't do anything about it, then no one is doing anything about it!"

Monroe pointed toward his teammates, who stood off to the side of the room, not quite supporting his brazen move but not taking a stand against it either.

"All of us down here at the bottom who know what's going on and can't get anybody to do anything about it just get more and more frustrated," he told Judd. "I'm speaking on behalf of all of us at the bottom of the chain of command."

"Once we get back on American soil, you are likely to be arrested for your insubordination, and I'll be powerless to stop it," Judd said.

"I don't care about insubordination," Monroe said. "I don't care if I lose my job. I don't care if you lock me up and throw away the key. I'll be safer in the brig than those girls are right now."

"You're going to lose everything, Captain." Judd shook his head with disdain. "You've thrown away your career."

"So be it. I will not stand back and let the Belizean government, or any government, turn a blind eye to people stealing little girls and raping them and creating pornography with their little bodies. These aren't adult women who are choosing to be prostitutes, Commander. These are little girls who are being stolen from their families and forced into prostitution long before their bodies are old enough to be having sex. These girls haven't even developed curves. They are little girls. You have a little girl. Wouldn't you do anything to protect her?"

"My daughter is five years old," Judd said. "That's not the same thing."

"Really? Have you seen the videos? There are girls in those pornography videos who are less than five years old. Ask Xavier. He's been dealing with this for years. There are babies in those pornography videos. There are kids of all ages. Boys and girls. These children are being exploited. If I know this is happening and I do nothing about it, then I am just as much at fault as the pedophiles and the rapists. And you, by standing here yelling at me right now, are adding to the problem. Are you a pedophile also?"

"How dare you!"

"How dare *you!*" Monroe yelled right back. "When you tuck your little girl into bed each night, remind yourself that there is a little girl somewhere in this world who is being tucked into bed by a man who is about to rape her. If you do nothing about it then you are as much a part of the problem as the rapist."

"That's a ridiculous comparison."

"Really? Because I bet those moms and dads who have had their children stolen from them also thought it was ridiculous"—Monroe pointed to the crowd outside the community center—"right up until the time their children were stolen from them. I pray to God that your children are never stolen from you, Commander."

"I pray that as well." His voice subdued, Judd looked down at the floor.

"God sends angels from mysterious places," Monroe said, lowering his voice with compassion. "And right now, you and I are the angels that are being sent to help these little girls who've been stolen. If standing in front of a microphone costs me my job but saves one little girl, then the sacrifice is worth it. So either get out of my way... or fire me."

With that, Monroe pushed past his superior officer and walked from the room.

Chapter Thirty-Nine

Thumbprint

"We had no idea this was happening." However dishonest, Prime Minister Nehemiah Paton of Belize spoke confidently into the microphone. He had called his own press conference and requested their guests from the United States Army to attend and sit in a place of honor. "Of course, we want to stop human trafficking."

The insincerity in his tone rubbed Monroe the wrong way. Yet something about the prime minister gave him pause. He remembered the allegations Joab had shared about how the Belizean government had been taken over by the military leader, Kaiah Amali. How Kaiah had brought a group of loyal supporters to the prime minister, as if to say they were his humble servants, then used that strength to take over control of the country. According to Joab, the prime minister didn't do anything without Kaiah whispering in his ear. Kaiah was even rumored to be having an affair with the prime minister's wife.

Nehemiah continued. "Unfortunately, most of the people purchasing slaves and pornography are from the United States of America. We call upon the U.S. government to fight against this evil. Nonetheless, we will do what we can here in Belize to stop the human traffickers."

"Gee, don't do us any favors," Monroe grumbled softly to his cousin, Henry, who sat at his side. Monroe fought the urge to fidget. He had been awake for over thirty-six hours, had left Florida and jumped out of an airplane to rescue teenagers near El Pilar on the contested border between Belize and Guatemala, had ruined his career and risked jail time by holding an impromptu and unauthorized press conference, and had flown by helicopter to Belmopan, the capital city of Belize. Now he had to sit through this blowhorn's lecture in the name of international collaboration. All he wanted was to drive across town to the U.S. Embassy where they could arrest him and tuck him into a nice, warm bed somewhere in the brig. Court-martial had never sounded so good.

"We have prepared a proclamation"—the prime minister held up a professional piece of parchment and waved it in the air—"stating that the Belizean government agrees to work with the United States government in the fight against child trafficking within the borders of our country. I will sign this now and hand the proclamation directly to the brave young soldier who took a stand earlier today."

The prime minister made a show of scrawling his signature across the page with an official-looking pen. Then he marched forward and looked Monroe in the eye. While handing the parchment to Monroe, the prime minister almost pulled the paper back out of his hand.

When Monroe glanced down at the paper, he realized that the prime minister had gripped the paper in such a way that he purposely created a noticeable thumbprint of black ink on the page. The intensity of his stare conveyed without words that there was a larger message on that parchment than merely a proclamation about human trafficking.

Monroe met his eye and tried to communicate that he'd understood the prime minister's unspoken request to analyze the parchment. He maintained a poker face as the prime minister strode back to his place of honor beside his military advisor, Kaiah Amali. Monroe fought the urge to narrow his eyes at the corrupt leader, remembering what Joab had said about the prime minister being a puppet to Kaiah Amali.

Monroe didn't mention the thumbprint to anyone until they'd driven to the embassy and found a private location with just his team, his cousins Henry and Aaron, and Xavier and Whitney from Operation Freedom Warriors.

"What's this all about?" Commander Judd Black asked. They all leaned over the page, staring at the thumbprint as if it held the clue to solving human trafficking.

"Maybe he wants us to dust the page for fingerprints because there's a hidden message on it." Monroe said.

"Paper can't be dusted for fingerprints," Judd said. "Maybe if you use superglue fumes."

"We'll try ultraviolet light, then," Monroe said. "There's more likely something written on there with invisible ink."

"You got all that from a thumbprint?" Brianna asked.

"Not just from the thumbprint," Monroe said. "It was more the look in his eyes trying to convey to me that there was more to the story."

Sure enough, when they analyzed the piece of paper under an ultraviolet light, there was a clearly written message on the back. The word *Help* along with a phone number and a time for later that evening. Great, this day just got longer.

Chapter Forty

A List of Names

"We don't have much time. If they have this room bugged, I'll be dead by morning." Prime Minister Nehemiah Paton of Belize wasted no time getting to his point. "When you called that press conference this morning, I jumped on the chance to communicate with you. I pulled together my cabinet and suggested we draft a formal declaration of peace and collaboration to placate the nosy Americans. Knowing they'd allow a formal delivery ceremony; I prepared the parchment with the hidden message."

"What is it you want?" Monroe asked. He had telephoned the number at the appointed time but needed the prime minister to clarify his request for help. Although Nehemiah had no guarantee he wasn't bugged on his end, Monroe and his team were most certainly recording this conversation from the security of the United States Embassy in Belmopan.

"All I want is justice. I'm devastated about what's happening to my people, and I want it stopped." Nehemiah was breathless trying to talk so fast. "I'm being controlled. They have bribed powerful people at all levels of the government and entered into backroom deals. The only reason I'm still in my position is because they think I'm going along with it. When in reality, I'm trying to figure out how to get out of this."

"What are you suggesting the United States do?" Monroe asked, glancing up at his commanding officer, Judd Black.

"I've made a list of everyone who is corrupt within my government, and I will give them to you verbally but not in writing. I'm not asking for favors in return, and I don't seek power. I just want my government back and for the corruption and human trafficking to stop."

"How do we know we can trust you?" Monroe asked.

"Because we both want what's good for the people, not for ourselves. If my military advisor, Kaiah Amali, finds out that I'm working with you, he will have me killed. I'm risking my life just talking to you. Like I said, if they have me bugged, I'll be dead by morning."

"Give us the names, and we'll see what we can do."

Thankfully they were recording the call because the prime minister spoke the names so quickly there was no way that Monroe could have written them all down. When he was done, Nehemiah took a deep breath and spoke from his heart.

"I'm so glad you're here. If I live or die, please keep up the fight until my people are safe. You can reach me at this phone number but only if it's an emergency. I may not be able to answer if I'm being watched. I pray that I live through this night."

"I pray that as well Mr. Prime Minister," Monroe said. "Thank you for your information. God bless you and God bless the people of Belize."

"Thank you, my young friend. God bless the United States of America for your help."

Monroe hung up the phone and met Commander Black's eye. "They're going to kill him if we don't get him out of there. If they do have him bugged, he'll be dead within the hour."

"He is not our responsibility," Judd said.

"The prime minister of a sovereign nation has asked for assistance from the United States, and we're in a position to help him. It would be inhumane not to rescue him. If he dies tonight, his blood will be on our hands."

"We don't even know where in his residence the prime minister is."

"Duchess will help us find him," Monroe said. That German shepherd had the nose of a bloodhound. "I'll call the prime minister back and tell him to hide somewhere near the helicopter pad on the roof of his residence, somewhere no one else would think to look for him. Duchess will find him."

Commander Black glanced around the room at the team, all who were alert and ready for action even though, like Monroe, they hadn't slept in almost two days.

"Maybe against my better judgement, I'll agree to this." Judd nodded. "I'll order a transport to get you in the sky. You'll need your night vision goggles, and sync your coms. You're landing on the roof of his residence, and we'll send a Pave Hawk to pick you up along with the prime minister... if he's still alive."

Chapter Forty-One

Duchess to the Rescue

Duchess didn't seem thrilled to be strapped against Monroe's chest while free-falling from a transport plane and then jerked to a halt when his parachute opened. They had a moment of reprieve as they floated to the earth, then a jolt when Monroe's feet hit the concrete roof of the prime minister's residence in Belmopan, Belize.

Monroe was always impressed with Duchess. She took her job seriously. She kept her team safe while on a mission. She knew how to check for explosives and drugs and find the bad guys or, in this case, the good guy. All they had to do was hold that parchment paper in front of her nose and set her loose. If a bad guy got in her way, she could take him down, hold him with her strong jaws, and wait until Monroe came to put the guy in cuffs. Oh yeah, she was good at her job.

Monroe unclipped Duchess from her harness, and her paws hit the concrete, dancing impatiently. She waited for the command, which was always in Dutch. They didn't want English speaking kids to say the wrong word or phrase and ask her to kill someone by mistake. As if she was that stupid. Monroe held the parchment in front of her nose again and said those magic words. Time to go find the guy who smelled like that paper.

Duchess led the team toward a door that opened to a stairway. She showed them the way to the bottom, then turned left and ran down the hallway.

She stopped in front of a door and sat outside, wagged her tail, and waited for Monroe to turn the knob.

A man cowered in the corner of the room, and Duchess hurried over and sat beside him, wagging her tail and looking up at Monroe.

"Good girl, Duchess." Monroe followed her into the room, rubbed her head and gave her a crunchy treat, then reached a hand down. "Mr. Prime Minister, let's get you to safety."

Prime Minister Nehemiah Paton reached up, and Monroe lifted him to his feet, towering over him. Sometimes Monroe forgot how large he was until he stood next to the leader of a democratically elected country and dwarfed the man standing next to him. There should be some unwritten rule that the head of state needs to be imposing and domineering. Then maybe he wouldn't get walked over by people like Kaiah Amali.

Monroe spoke into his com. "This is Alpha One. I've secured the prime minister."

"How quickly can you get him onto the roof?" Brianna asked through the com.

"Less than five minutes if everything's clear between here and the staircase."

"We've got a Pave Hawk en route to your location and should be able to land as soon as you can get there."

"Copy that." Before Monroe and Nehemiah reached the door to the room, Brianna's voice rang through the com again.

"Be advised, we are picking up a single heat signature on the second floor of the prime minister's residence," Brianna said. "You've got company."

"Let's move." Monroe spoke more quietly but insistent. "Someone's looking for you."

Alpha team surrounded the prime minister and escorted him to the stairway leading up to the helipad.

"Your position is compromised," Brianna called. "Multiple heat signatures are now lighting up the second floor and rapidly approaching your position." In this maze of hallways, they could be anywhere, and the team wouldn't know until they were standing face-to-face.

"We need immediate extraction. Get that helicopter on the roof!"

"Inbound. ETA two minutes," Brianna said.

"Split up and cover the hallway from both ends," Monroe told his team.

Raymond and Blake hurried down the hallway past the door where they would eventually ascend the stairs to the helipad. Stone and Davis surrounded Nehemiah as if they were his secret service detail and hurried to the open door leading to the roof.

Two minutes seemed an eternity when waiting in dark silence, not knowing which of the alcoves ahead was a doorway and which was a hallway leading to another part of the second floor. He wished they'd had time to memorize the schematics of the floorplan before doing this mission.

Splitting up turned out to be a bad idea. None of them knew where the others were and none of them knew who was around the next corner, friend or foe, housekeeper or hired hitman.

Finally, the unmistakable whir of the Pave Hawk came from above and chaos broke loose. A bullet whizzed past Monroe from an alcove between him and the staircase leading to the roof.

"I'll cover you. Get the prime minister into that helicopter now!" Monroe didn't dare shoot back at whoever was around that corner because he could see from his vantage point that his team was still in the hallway and just reaching the door to the staircase. He could count that they were all there, including Duchess.

Then the door closed, and Monroe breathed a sigh of relief that his team was safe. Getting himself to safety was a different matter. He didn't know how many guys were still on the second floor or whether they knew he was there. Monroe barely took a breath for several minutes, considering his options.

"Alpha One, what is your position?" Raymond asked through the com. "The team is loaded and ready to get off this pad. Where are you?"

"I'm not going to make it back to the roof. There are shooters between me and you. Get out now, and come back for me!"

"We're not leaving you behind, Captain!"

"Get the prime minister to safety, and then come back for me. That's an order!"

There was a flurry of voices in protest. Finally, Monroe heard the helicopter leave the roof and knew he was alone.

As the Pave Hawk flew away, an eerie silence blanketed the hallway. Monroe didn't dare move. He could hear Brianna's frantic voice through the com, but he couldn't answer for fear he'd give away his position.

"Alpha One, I don't know if you can hear me, but you still have a total of four heat signatures all holding their position on alert on the second floor of the residence. They likely know at least one of you is on that floor, but they don't have intel on your location."

Monroe desperately wished he could communicate to Brianna that he was alive and well and give her an idea which heat signature belonged to him. Then he realized he could. His homing device was within reach, and he clicked the button to sound the alert that he needed assistance. The helicopter was returning for him anyway, but this would give a clear signal.

Unfortunately, the click of the button on the homing device was enough to alert the shooters of his general location and bullets flew past his head again. He tucked himself as far into the alcove as he could, knowing if he moved one inch forward, he'd be exposed.

A gunshot was louder the second round, and a man fell forward, his gun falling from his hand and a red stain spreading on the back of his white shirt. Who shot the guy that fell?

Raymond? Monroe could see down the hall that Ray had stepped into the hallway near the door leading to the roof and had his gun trained in this direction. Guess Monroe hadn't been as alone as he'd thought.

"Nice shot, Two," Monroe said in a loud whisper, knowing Ray would hear him through the com but not risking any other shooters knowing his location.

"Thanks, One, now get down here so we can head home."

"There's still at least one other shooter on this floor," Monroe told him, then turned his attention to Brianna. "Lieutenant Turner, now that you know where Ray and I are, where's the other heat signature?"

"Unfortunately, in between the two of you."

"What's the ETA on that Hawk?"

"A little over one minute," she said.

"I'll wait to leave my position until we hear that bird land, and then I'm just going to have to hope Ray gets the shooter before the shooter gets me."

"We have the advantage of night vision, Captain," Raymond said. "I doubt he does."

Twenty seconds later, the whir of the Pave Hawk approached, and Monroe prepared to leave his position.

"Alpha Two, I'm going to step into the hallway, drawing fire, then I'll step back into the alcove so you can take this guy out. I'm ready for a hot bath and a good night's sleep back at the embassy, how about you?"

"Affirmative, Alpha One. On your count."

"Three... two... one." Monroe stepped into the hallway and then immediately back. A bullet clipped his sleeve. Then another shot rang out, and the man fell to the floor near his buddy.

Monroe didn't wait around to see if the guy was alive or dead. He just ran as fast as he could to where Raymond was holding open the door to the staircase leading to the roof. They bolted the door behind themselves and pounded up the stairs. Without looking back, they made a beeline for the waiting helicopter and jumped into the open cabin. The bird lifted off the roof, and Monroe reached out a fist to his best friend. "Thanks for having my six."

"You knew I wouldn't leave you behind, you idiot." Raymond bumped his fist, and they both chuckled. One more rescue carried out for the day. Only fourteen more to go.

Chapter Forty-Two

Willpower

One hour. That's all it would take to quench this frustration. Way less than that. Heck, they could duck into the restroom off the kitchenette and be done before anyone realized they were together.

All the sexual tension between them would be gone.

No, that was a lie. Like a single hit of heroin, Monroe would want more. And more. And more. Just holding Brianna in his arms like this was setting him nearly over the edge.

Monroe didn't hesitate to pull her close even though he knew they were standing in full view of anyone who might walk down the dark hallway, however unlikely.

After the team debriefing, everyone had dispersed. Since they'd arrived at the United States Embassy after midnight, members of the team were taken to rooms where they could stay for the night and regroup in the morning.

Before heading to the room where he'd sleep, Monroe walked down the hall to a kitchenette lounge where he found more food than he had in his apartment back home. Before he could take a full inventory of all the choices of snacks and cereals and beverages and chips and crackers and fruit, Brianna snuck into the room and wrapped her arms around his waist.

Now they held each other while a fire burned between them.

"I was so worried about you." Brianna's sultry voice pierced into Monroe's core, and she squeezed his waist just a little tighter, holding him as if she'd never let go. "You can't do that ever again."

"I didn't have a choice," he whispered fiercely. "We had to get the prime minister to safety. He was the priority."

"Yeah, well, *you* are my priority," Brianna said.

"See, that's why two members of the same team aren't supposed to fall in love." Monroe pulled back slightly and lifted his hands to smooth back the tendrils of hair that had fallen loose from her braids. "Because decisions in the field can't be made based on emotions. They have to be automatic."

"Is that what we're doing?" The vulnerability in her eyes was endearing. "Falling in love?"

Loaded question. "I don't know. Love, lust, passion, attraction, whatever you want to call this. All I know is that, since the first time I looked at you across the bar, you've been like a siren to me. And then when you needed me to rescue you from Stone hitting on you, that was my excuse to get close to you. Guys want to feel *needed*."

Monroe didn't mean to pull her even closer, but he did. And he liked feeling her flush against his body.

"You intrigue me, Brianna." His breathing was heavy as he gazed down at her. "Your confidence as a woman and as an officer, the way you command attention whenever you walk in a room, whatever perfume you wear, and don't get me started on your voice. Having you talk me through these ops, your words penetrate right through the coms and into my soul."

"Will you please just kiss me and get it over with?" Brianna lifted her face to his, expecting him to lean down and connect his lips to hers.

"No." Rather than kissing her lips, he leaned down and kissed her neck just below her right ear, then moved to the other side and kissed her neck below her left ear. "I will not kiss you."

"You just did," she whispered, her body slack in his muscled arms. "Twice."

"Not the way I want to." His voice was low and husky.

"Why?" she pleaded with desperation in her voice. "Why won't you kiss me the way you want to?"

"Because I will *not* want to stop." Monroe laced his fingers into Brianna's hair, gripping her head with passion and longing, kissing her neck and cheeks and forehead and then back down to her neck, avoiding her mouth.

"Then don't stop," she said with a growl, pulling him closer.

"We can't be together, Brianna." His whisper caressed her name the way he wished he could caress her body. "We can't let this happen." Even as he spoke, he lifted her into his arms, and she wrapped her legs around his waist. He continued to kiss her everywhere except her lips.

"Please?" She kept forcing her lips closer to his, and he was losing the will to deny her. "One kiss?"

One kiss. What could it hurt? One passionate, incredible kiss, and then he would walk away.

His resolve crumbled, and his lips met hers with a hunger he'd never experienced. With her still wrapped around him like a monkey, he pressed her against the wall, forcing their bodies even closer together.

How effortlessly he could finish this. How badly he wanted to allow his body to make that final decision. When Brianna reached for the top button of his shirt, that woke him up, and he pulled away and set her on the floor with controlled insistence.

Where in the fabric of his DNA he found the willpower to pull away from her, he'll never know. But somehow, Monroe placed one final kiss on Brianna's lips and backed away, shaking his head.

"I'm sorry. I won't risk your career, and I can't stop being who I am," Monroe said, taking another step back. "I'm Alpha One. My team needs me to lead them, and I have a job to do. You and I both have jobs to do, and those jobs prevent us from being together. If I allow myself to fall in love with you... I'll love you forever."

With that passionate declaration, Captain Monroe Cohen performed the most impossible feat of his life. He walked away from Lieutenant Brianna Turner.

Chapter Forty-Three

Following All the Rules

Monroe was awakened to a pounding on his bedroom door and, for a moment, couldn't remember where he was. Oh yeah. The United States embassy in Belize.

Last night they had rescued the prime minister and afterward he had kissed Brianna with more passion than he knew possible. He rolled over in bed with a smile and groaned audibly at the thought of never kissing her again. He was right in thinking she'd be like a drug to him. He already wanted another fix.

The pounding on his door snapped him back from fantasizing about the woman of his dreams.

"What?" Monroe called out to whoever was so bold as to disturb what little sleep he'd had in three days. The door opened, and Commander Judd Black entered. Had the door been unlocked? Or did his commanding officer have a key?

"Kaiah Amali has fled the capital city along with several of his closest friends, all of whose names were on the prime minister's list."

"Good morning to you too, Commander." Monroe sat up in bed, exposing his bare chest. Assuming Judd wouldn't want to see him in his boxers, Monroe left the blankets over his lower half. "Please say you brought me something with caffeine."

Judd ignored Monroe's sarcasm and continued. "They must have figured out that the prime minister planned to expose them. We have a five-minute lag between satellite images showing them leaving. That's as close to real-time data as we can get over foreign soil. Kind of helps having the head of state giving permission to use their satellites."

"A lot can happen in five minutes." Monroe yawned and stretched but continued his impromptu briefing. "Any idea where they're heading?"

"Belize City, most likely. If we can keep eyes on them, they might lead us toward someone with connections to the human trafficking ring. We already have eyes on the ground near the entrance to the city thanks to our contacts with Operation Freedom Warriors."

"How soon do we head out? Got a Hawk available to give us a lift?"

"Fueled up and ready to go as soon as you get out of bed."

"Get out of my room, and I'll get out of bed." Monroe raised his eyebrows.

"Who's still in bed?" Stone poked his head in the door. Great, more company. "You lazy dog."

Blake pushed Stone all the way into the room. "Don't bug the captain. He needs his beauty sleep."

Raymond and Davis also stopped at Monroe's open door on their way to wherever it was they were going. Guess the gang's all awake.

The next person to walk in the door was Brianna, and she stopped short, gaping at Monroe, who still sat up in bed, naked from the waist up. Her jaw dropped as her eyes scanned his torso. "Dang!" Brianna clapped her hand over her mouth and hurried away. Oops.

"That doesn't change the status of whether or not she's seen me naked, does it?" Monroe joked with his commanding officer. All the guys snickered.

"Anything I should know about?" Judd folded his arms across his chest and raised his eyebrows.

"Nope." Monroe left his one-word answer hang in the air.

"Watch yourself," Judd warned.

"I'm gonna watch myself right over to a cold shower as soon as you see yourself out of my room," Monroe answered.

Judd grunted and pulled the door shut as he left, taking Monroe's audience with him.

Monroe grumbled under his breath as he gathered the clothes he'd strewn on the floor the night before. "A very, very cold shower."

The guys razzed him the minute he strode into the briefing room, commenting on his wet hair, his rumpled uniform, and the way Monroe and Brianna were avoiding eye contact.

They tried taking jabs at Brianna, but she was too quick. "And I thought he looked good in his uniform. Might have to change my mind about our relationship status." He could tell she was teasing for the team's sake but there was an underlying message to him that her teasing was a ruse to hide her true feelings.

He decided to add a jab of his own. "As long as I haven't seen *her* naked, we're still following all the rules."

"You haven't followed any rules in two days. Why start now?" Judd showed a tiny hint of a smile, and Monroe jumped on his guard being down.

"Now, see, babe, we got permission from our commanding officer. Let's go. My room's just down the hall."

"Very funny." Brianna was all business now, but the warning look she gave Monroe told him they weren't through with that conversation. She changed the subject and shifted to game mode, calling out to the guys. "Gentlemen, we have updated intel showing Kaiah Amali and his cohorts entering Belize City, and one of the freedom warriors is trailing them."

A giant map appeared on the big screen, with real-time updates and better surveillance within the city.

"We think they're heading for this section of town with the shipping and loading docks." Brianna used her pointer to show the location. "Prime Minister Paton has obtained permission for us to land on the helipad at the local hospital, right here." She moved her pointer.

Judd piped in. "The hospital is only a few blocks from the freedom warriors' temporary headquarters. Hopefully by the time we get to Belize City, they'll have Kaiah Amali and his buddies pinned down."

"I don't need to overstate this, gentlemen, but we need stealth with this operation," Brianna said. "Although we have permission from the head of state, we are not in contact with local government units, and we need to keep it that way. If these guys have anyone on the inside there in Belize City, we'll be compromised and Kaiah Amali will spook."

"What are our orders, Lieutenant?" Monroe asked. "Are we taking these guys into custody? Or eliminating them? Are we sanctioned to look for the missing girls? Or do we still have our hands tied behind our backs?"

Judd broke in. "That is going to be left to your discretion in the field, Captain. If you think you can find those girls while you're down at the loading docks, there won't be any of us there to tell you otherwise."

Monroe raised his eyebrows subtly at his commanding officer, and Judd raised his right back with a tiny smirk. Monroe made a vow to himself right then and there to move heaven and earth to find those girls. This was his one shot.

Chapter Forty-Four

Phone Calls to the Enemy

A quick ride in a helicopter brought them to the roof of the hospital in Belize City, a resort town on the Caribbean Sea where the uber-rich park their yachts in the north end of town and the criminals ship their drugs and girls from the south pier. That was where Alpha team was heading with the guys from Operation Freedom Warriors.

But first the team was escorted to the freedom warriors' makeshift head-quarters—a fancy house on the beach—tucked discreetly in the richest part of the city. They didn't want the traffickers to question how the warriors could afford to purchase all these girls. They always had rich American friends showing up in gleaming white yachts with deep pockets and sadistic appetites. Or so the traffickers thought.

Several of the freedom warriors had gotten in close with the traffickers to the point where they had identified the top dogs and were preparing a takedown. This was the perfect opportunity to strike.

Aside from having a Special Forces team operating on very little sleep, there were several other challenges. There were too many angles to consider at once.

They had fourteen missing girls from the Mayan tribe, a corrupt gov-ernment official on the run who needed to be stopped, several human trafficking rings to find and take down—each with little cells that operate independently of each other—and no idea which group had the Mayan girls in their custody.

The question was how many of those angles could they tackle in one day?

Taking down even one of the human trafficking rings could make a difference. But Monroe wanted to find those Mayan girls.

Kaiah Amali had been followed to a seedy part of town before the freedom warriors lost his trail. He slipped between two warehouses near the shipping containers and could be parked in any of the docking bays. The freedom warriors were nervous they would reveal themselves if they poked their noses around too much. They staked out near the entrance to the docks.

"We don't exactly have a lot of intelligence to go on," Monroe said, feeling the gravity of the situation.

"Actually, we do," Xavier said with confidence. Standing among several others of his warriors, Xavier seemed more in his element than he had while at the Mayan reservation. "We've been working this area for a long time, and we already have guys in their inner circles. Parker can organize a party for this afternoon." Xavier indicated a man on his right, a sculpted powerhouse who looked as if he could intimidate a mob boss.

"What do you mean by a party?" Monroe asked. Maybe he was functioning on too little sleep to understand why the freedom warriors would want to throw a party. He glanced longingly at the plush sofa gracing the sculpted carpeting of this stylish beach house. Heck, as tired as he was, he could probably bypass the sofa and fall asleep on the elegant carpeting.

"A sex party." Parker's terse statement had an implied *duh* on the end. "I'm simultaneously these guys' biggest client and worst nightmare."

"Yeah, I could see how you'd be a little intimidating." Monroe offered a half-hearted chuckle and Parker smirked at him.

"Make some phone calls, Parker," Xavier said. "Show these boys how it's done."

Parker touched the screen of his smart phone a few times, then held the phone in front of him while the speaker rang out and a guy answered after the second ring.

"Parker, mi amigo. ¿Cómo estás?" A man's voice greeted Parker, but he didn't waste time with salutations. He got right down to the business of the call.

"Philip, I've got some guys from America coming in on a yacht later today, and they want to have a party. Got anything new?"

"For you? Always," Philip answered through the speaker phone. "How young?"

"Not too young," Parker said. "Teenage girls, maybe?"

"Got lots to choose from." Philip sounded excited.

"Virgins." Parker's insistence was not a question.

"Now that's gonna cost you extra," Philip said.

"These guys are loaded. That's not going to be a problem."

"I'll see what I can provide."

"I'm coming down your way in about an hour. Have a selection for me to choose from."

"An hour?" Philip's voice rose an octave.

"You need me to delay my arrival?" Parker asked in a way that indicated he was annoyed by the need to be flexible. "I can wait an extra half hour or so."

"If you want virgins, you've gotta give me time," Philip said.

"Two hours," Parker demanded. "Not a minute longer. I'll meet you at our regular spot." With that, he hung up the phone.

"Do you think he actually has the girls we're looking for?" Monroe asked.

"Doesn't matter." Parker shrugged. "With your billionaire prince financing this sting, we can afford to buy them all. Plus, I've got four more guys to call. We're gonna get busy this afternoon."

Parker held up his phone and dialed the next number on his list. After four similar conversations, Parker had scheduled five purchases to go down simultaneously at the same location. The traffickers were familiar with Parker's mode of operating. He claimed he wanted the best selection, and they all showed up with their hands out displaying the finest kidnapped girls they could find.

Because Aaron had arranged a special delivery by way of a private jet, he had secured $100,000 in cash delivered to the embassy the previous day. Seed money to take down multiple human trafficking rings. Must be nice to snap one's fingers and have cash flown down from New York. But money wasn't the only thing needed to pull off the arrests of that many people.

When Monroe and his cousins had shown their faces at the press conference, they had taken themselves out of consideration for direct contact with the traffickers, but they would be assisting the Belizean government in the raid.

Rescuing the prime minister had proven to be the final piece needed in a very methodical and long-range plan. Prime Minister Nehemiah Paton had provided four of his most trusted secret service agents and permission to take these traffickers down.

The local group of ten freedom warriors had been expanded and strengthened by six Special Forces guys from the United States military, plus the four Belizean secret service agents. If that amount of firepower couldn't take down five human trafficking rings, nothing could.

Chapter Forty-Five

Pure Evil

A sting operation involved weeks, sometimes months of stakeout for reconnaissance and positioning. The staff from Operation Freedom Warriors had bugged this warehouse weeks ago and had livestream video from all angles. The building also had many places for warriors to hunker down and wait for the signal to move in. Monroe was positioned with a full view of the large room where the transaction would take place.

Henry had been joined by the oldest of the Mayan teenage boys, Machudo, who claimed he was Henry's second in command. Monroe suspected the young man had some higher ulterior motive. One of the girls perhaps? A sister or a girlfriend? The intensity of his involvement went beyond just wanting to help rescue his tribal members. This time, instead of rifles, crossbows, and hunting knives, Machudo had been trained to handle a Beretta 9mm. Instead of a T-shirt, the kid had full Kevlar armor like the rest of the team. This girl he was trying to rescue wouldn't recognize him.

Everyone had been warned to brace themselves for the onslaught of evil they were about to encounter. The freedom warriors were trained as undercover operatives to act, talk, and behave like a pedophile. They would probably do and say things very unbecoming to an officer and a gentleman.

As if to fortify themselves from this darkness, the warriors gathered together for a heartfelt prayer meeting just before leaving for any op. The moment had been touching, and Monroe reminded himself of the conversation he'd had with his commanding officer the prior day about God sending angels. These freedom warriors embodied God's angels. They were truly impressive.

Now hunkered down in this dank warehouse, Monroe tried to pull that same spirit into his present environment, and it wasn't easy. Especially as pimps and girls started arriving. He watched the men push the girls into lines like cattle at the business end of a prod. He heard the f-bomb used as an adjective, verb, noun, and adverb, sometimes within the same sentence. They discussed the ages of the girls as if each one was a prize to be taken. Thirteen, fifteen, sixteen. There was one girl who claimed to be eighteen but was obviously younger. One little girl unashamedly told Parker she was eleven. Monroe wanted to throw up.

"Hey, Philip," Parker called out to one of the pimps. "This little slut is *not* a virgin. What are you trying to pull?"

"How do you know she is not?" Philip's question was spoken with fake innocence. "Did she lie to me?"

"I can just tell by looking into her eyes." Parker pulled the teenage girl closer and rubbed his hand up her back. "She knows how to make me feel good. Don't you, baby?"

Her answer was too soft for Monroe to hear but accompanied by a seductive giggle.

"Oh, you'd like that, wouldn't you?" Parker asked, tightening his grip around her. "How old are you, baby?"

"Fifteen," she said with more flirting. The girl pulled her shoulders back, exposing as much cleavage as her tiny little girl body could boast, and Parker purposely looked down her shirt.

"You're just the perfect age, aren't you?" Parker lifted his gaze to Philip. "I'll take her too, but don't try to charge me. And next time be certain what merchandise you have on display." Parker released the underage girl from his arms as if he were discarding a tissue and kept walking down the line.

"Honest mistake." Philip waved off Parker's concerns. "Won't happen again."

"Is this all you got?" Parker turned and wrapped an arm around the slimy pimp's shoulder and pulled him a little closer. "I heard you got in a shipment of little beauties from over in Guatemala."

"Nah, man, that was Gonzalez," Philip said.

Parker dropped his arm from around Philip's shoulders and stepped away. "Good, he should be here soon. I have lots of money. I'll keep looking at what you've got here while we're waiting."

Monroe wanted to be optimistic about Gonzalez showing up but had a nervous prick in the back of his mind. Maybe he was just feeling disgust from watching this God-fearing man, who had been praying fervently an hour ago, walk along a line of girls, leer at them, touch their arms and necks, and run his fingers through their hair. Parker returned twice to that fifteen-year-old who he claimed wasn't a virgin. All the interaction was part of the diversion tactics but nauseating to watch.

More pimps arrived with more girls and the warehouse got fuller and louder. Finally, the man they were all waiting for sauntered in, followed by about a dozen girls. Monroe wasn't sure how he could tell the difference, but he suspected these were Belizean runaways rather than stolen Mayan girls.

"Gonzalez!" Parker called out to him as if they were old friends. He simultaneously singled Gonzalez out to all the hidden cameras, established a less-formal cadence, and hoisted the pompous jerk onto a metaphorical pedestal. But when Parker pulled Gonzalez aside to ask about the new girls, he played dumb as if he had no idea who Parker was talking about.

Parker's demeanor shifted, and he gathered the pimps together in a huddle, drawing them closer to where Monroe was hiding. Time to get down to business.

"I know you're all going to match each other's prices anyway so let's just fix that right up front and agree each girl is worth $500 a piece for the remainder of the day. That's a generous price considering they're *not all virgins*." Parker looked pointedly at Philip. "Are we in accord?"

The pimps all nodded, high-fived and fist bumped, bartering for the lives of young girls. The whole scenario was sickening.

"I've got the money right here," Parker said, opening a briefcase full of cash. He counted out stacks of thousands, giving a few thousand to each guy and then started around to give more thousands. Each pimp needed to receive enough money that they could be busted for selling girls, but not the entire amount on the first go round. The team needed the pimps to have their hands out and their guards down.

And that was the signal to move in. Time to arrest some cockroaches. Monroe couldn't wait. If only the Mayan girls had been here.

Chapter Forty-Six

You Deserve Better than This

"Execute, execute, execute!" Monroe called out.

They entered the large warehouse from all sides, coming out of the woodwork where they'd been hiding, guns trained on the traffickers, including Parker, as was the norm. He would allow himself to be arrested along with everyone else.

"Which one of you called the cops?" Parker yelled, along with a stream of obscenities. "You idiots." Again, Monroe had a difficult time associating this crass individual with the man who had been praying an hour ago at the Operation Freedom Warriors headquarters.

"Get down on the ground," Monroe shouted. "Now!" He held his gun to Parker's head, very uncomfortable with the situation and wishing he wasn't working with live ammo.

Others on his team were apprehending the traffickers, wrapping their wrists with zip ties and forcing them onto the ground.

Adrenaline raced through Monroe's veins for all thirty seconds it took to tie up the five main guys plus the four others that had come with the pimps.

This had been too easy. Something was wrong. Xavier was angry and yelling at Gonzalez, "Where are the Mayan girls?"

"I don't know, I don't know," Gonzalez insisted.

"Liar!" Xavier shoved Gonzalez hard into the ground. "Tell me where they are! What you say in the next thirty seconds is going to determine how you'll spend the next thirty years of your life! Now tell me where they are!"

"On the pier," Gonzalez cried. "I sold them to a guy an hour ago. They're in a shipping crate on the pier, waiting to be loaded. They might have already been loaded."

"Where is this pier?" Machudo stepped forward, anger and horror clouding his judgement. If he'd known the location, there was no doubt he'd already be running in that direction.

"I'll take you there in a minute," Xavier said and then turned to his team of freedom warriors. "Half of you, get these guys processed. The other half of you, come with me to the pier. We have more traffickers to arrest and fourteen more girls to rescue."

"Wait," Parker called to Xavier from where he was tied up next to the pimps. "Take off my restraints. I need to say something to these girls."

Xavier shook his head and sighed, resigned that one of his undercover operatives would no longer be able to serve undercover now that he'd revealed himself to the traffickers. Some of them would likely be out on bond within a few days and back in business. He took out a pocketknife and sliced through the zip tie.

Parker hopped onto his feet, then jogged across the room to where the aftercare team was already tending to the dozens of terrified girls. He headed straight for the fifteen-year-old girl he'd called a slut.

"I'm sorry for the way I treated you. All of you." Parker took a moment to look around, meeting the gazes of several other girls. "No man should ever be allowed to treat you the way these men did, and the way I did. You're all beautiful in God's eyes and deserve to be treated like ladies. These women will take good care of you and get you to safety. Okay?"

The aftercare facilities were ready to accept as many girls as the team could purchase, and from what Monroe could see there were at least three dozen teenage girls here.

Again, Parker focused on the fifteen-year-old girl. "Your body is sacred and special. No man should ever look down your shirt like I did and for that I apologize. These women will help you find some more modest clothing so that won't happen to you again. God bless you. God bless all of you." Parker glanced around the group again then ran back over to be with his team.

Monroe was certain Parker had tears welling up in his eyes, but no one called him out. There inevitably comes a time in a guy's life when something breaks, and he can no longer hold himself together. Everyone understood, and all of them looked away as if they had important business anywhere other than meeting Parker's gaze.

"Let's move," Xavier called out. "We have more work to do."

Everyone who had been assigned to head to the docks followed Xavier, and they all climbed into three waiting Suburbans.

The warehouse where they'd rescued the girls was less than a mile from the pier, that is, it was a mile from the entrance to the pier. Once at the entrance, there was over a quarter mile drive down a long, thin bridge jutting out into the Caribbean Sea. The drive would be nerve racking under normal circumstances. With stakes this high, Monroe's nerves were ready to snap.

With white knuckles, their driver, one of the freedom warriors, pulled onto the narrow bridge and crept forward. Monroe reminded himself that semi-trucks carrying shipping containers traversed this bridge multiple times a day, and if truck drivers could do this, so could three Suburbans.

Shipping containers. Is that what Gonzales had meant when he said the girls were in a shipping crate on the pier? Waiting to be loaded? Loaded onto what? An ocean freighter container ship? Heading where?

Monroe had a bad feeling about this.

Chapter Forty-Seven

Rich and Powerful Men

The guys from the prime minister's security detail were as good as customs officers. One flash of their badges was all it took to gain access to the freighter that was docked at the end of the pier.

Finding the girls was another story. There were hundreds of forty-foot shipping containers on that freighter, and the crew members on the ship had no idea what, or who, was inside each container. Or so they claimed.

Monroe suspected that someone on this boat knew where the girls were. He met the gaze of each crew member, evaluating their level of honesty. Finally, he came to one guy who seemed shifty. Monroe didn't hesitate or pretend they were on the freighter for a random inspection. He strode right over and towered over the man.

"Where are the Mayan girls?" Monroe's voice was menacing in its lack of emotion. He wasn't asking *if* the guy knew where the Mayan girls were. Monroe was stating definitively that he knew the man was privy to their location.

"I don't know what you're talking about." The man seemed a little too well dressed to be a dock worker or a crewmember on the ship.

Monroe decided to take a page from Xavier's playbook. "What you say in the next thirty seconds will determine how you spend the next thirty years of your life."

His statement didn't have the same effect on this man as it did on Gonzales. "The only thing I'm going to say to you is that you can search every last one of these containers and you ain't gonna find no Mayan girls."

"Is that so?" Monroe searched his eyes. The man was telling the truth. Weird. He didn't even look worried or scared of Monroe even though Monroe towered over the kid.

Not in any of the *containers*. The man said they could search every *container* and not find the girls. Which meant those girls were somewhere else on the ship. He turned and met Xavier's eyes then directed his statement to one of the prime minister's personal security detail.

"Get the customs officer out here. We're searching every square inch of this freighter until we find those girls."

"Hey, man, I've got a schedule and deadlines." A different man put his hand on Monroe's arm. Monroe glanced down at the man's hand, and he pulled away. "You can't just hold up my departure because you're looking for some runaways."

"Are you the buyer?" Monroe asked, not backing down.

"The what?" The man's voice cracked with nervousness. Yeah, he was guilty too.

"You know, the buyer." Monroe was losing his temper. "The cockroach who likes to play with little girls and buys them and sells them at the next port."

"I don't know what you're talking about."

"Funny, that's what your buddy over here said too." Monroe hitched his thumb at the other crewmember. "Is there anything you *do* know?"

The man just pursed his lips.

"Look, we can do this the easy way—you can hand over the girls and leave this dock and make it to your destination on time—or we can do this the hard way. Which would you prefer?"

Monroe sensed two individuals step up behind him and didn't need to turn to know his cousin, Henry, was at his left shoulder and Raymond was on his right. In his peripheral vision, he saw Xavier stand beside Raymond, and Henry's young friend, Machudo, flanked him on his left.

"Please, sir." Machudo stepped forward. "I want my future wife back. We were to be married next Saturday. She and her sister were stolen from our village along with several other girls. Fourteen are still missing. If you know where they are, please tell us."

The man's face softened, and he met the gazes of the row of intimidating men in front of him. "I'm not the buyer, but I think I know where the girls are. A couple hours ago, four men showed up with their daughters and asked if we could help get them out of the country. They paid our ship's captain some money for no-questions-asked stowaway status. They're probably down in the cargo hold."

"Would you please take us there?" Monroe asked through clenched teeth, trying to follow Machudo's example and appeal to the man's humanity.

"I don't want to get into trouble with our captain." The guy hesitated.

"You'll be in a lot more trouble if we call in the customs officers," Monroe said, counting on his fingers. "Harboring a criminal, four counts; kidnapping, fourteen counts; transporting stolen goods, fourteen counts—"

"Okay, okay, I get it. Follow me." The man turned and led the way to a set of stairs.

An endless set of stairs. There were nine floors on the ship, and apparently the crew leader had no intention of offering the assistance of an elevator. Monroe wanted to shout at the guy that they didn't need a tour of all nine decks. They just wanted to find the girls.

When they reached the lowest level, they were led down endless passageways. Monroe started to wonder if this little tour was a diversion to throw them off course. Were they being led into an ambush? Were the girls even on the ship, or was this guy setting them up?

"Huh... I would have thought they would have been harbored down here in the cargo hold." The crew leader stopped at another dead end and scratched his head. He turned and faced Monroe. "They wouldn't have been taken to the officers' quarters, would they?"

"You tell me." Monroe stepped closer, once again towering over the man.

"They'd have to be some pretty rich and powerful men to have convinced the captain to let them on board, right?" the crew leader ruminated. "Maybe he did invite them to his quarters." The man turned and pushed past Monroe, heading back the way they'd come.

Monroe didn't have any choice other than to follow. Several floors back up, they found themselves on a deck that was much nicer than the others. If this container ship were a luxury cruise liner, this would be first class. Where everything else on the ship was industrial, this area was plush and elegant. The air even smelled better.

But even the finery couldn't stop the hairs on Monroe's neck from standing on end, as if he inherently knew they were close.

He was right.

The crew leader opened a gilded door into a lounge area where multiple men sat on low sofas, propping up their feet and laughing as if they hadn't a care in the world. One man had a commanding presence, and Monroe pegged him as the ship's captain. Several other men were his officers, the rest of the men wore business suits. All of the men had at least one teenage girl sitting on their laps or tucked up next to them.

And the central figure in the room, with one girl on each knee, was Kaiah Amali himself.

"Well, well, well," Monroe said. "Funny we should find you here."

The smile fell from Kaiah's face as realization replaced his shock. He'd been caught trying to flee the country, after purchasing kidnapped, underage girls.

Monroe's satisfaction upon finding two of the objects of their search at the same time was short-lived as he heard the unmistakable click of a handgun beside his temple.

Chapter Forty-Eight

Kaiah Amali

Machudo pushed past Monroe as if he had no idea of the danger. He probably didn't. His innocent, peaceful life on the Mayan reservation had protected him from having to witness the kind of horror that existed in the world outside his forest.

One of the girls not snuggled up beside a man rose from the sofa and raced into Machudo's arms bathing his face in kisses.

"You're here to rescue me! You're here to rescue me," she said in Spanish, over and over.

"I'm sorry it took me so long to find you," Machudo said, kissing her face as she kissed his.

The scene would have been more touching if Monroe didn't have a gun to his head. He didn't dare move or turn his head to see who held the gun.

He took inventory of those who were in the room. Kaiah and all of his cronies, the captain, some officers, the crew leader who had led them on the tour of the ship, and fourteen girls were all within view. So who had the gun to his head?

Monroe chanced a sidelong glance and found the well-dressed crew member that Monroe had pegged as guilty.

The smirk on the jerk's face was aggravating.

Monroe could have easily apprehended the gun from the man's hand, but he wasn't sure how many other people in the room also had guns and whether or not they would retaliate.

Based on the way the man's hand was shaking with nervousness, it was highly unlikely that he would actually pull the trigger.

"Leo, what are you doing?" The man who had led them through the ship was gaping at his shipmate, who still had a gun to Monroe's head.

"This is none of your concern, Teagan," Leo said. "I'm just taking a little insurance policy with me to the next port."

"I am your superior officer on this ship, and I order you to stand down," Teagan said.

"Well, I'm the captain of this ship." The confident captain stood, pushing aside the two teenage girls on his lap. "And I order you to keep the gun trained on this cocky Navy SEAL."

"I am *not* a Navy SEAL," Monroe said. He would never presume to take on such distinction. Monroe was proud of his commission in the Army as a Special Forces Airborne Ranger and knew his rank of captain was impressive. But a SEAL is a cut above even the rangers. There was a high level of respect through all the branches of the military for such an elite group of men.

"I don't care what you are, Mister High-and-Mighty," the ship's captain said. "You're on my ship now, and you have no authority here."

"Oh, I'm pretty sure international law says otherwise." Monroe chuckled, amazed at how calm he was surrounded by corrupt and evil individuals and still at gunpoint. "No matter where your ship is docked, it's still illegal to kidnap little girls and use them for sex."

"Do any of us look like we're having sex?" Kaiah Amali stood and flexed his upper body as if trying to prove he could take Monroe down in a fist fight.

"I think possession with intent would apply here," Monroe said. "We have evidence that you paid for these girls, and that alone is illegal. So how about if you hand over the girls, and y'all can sail off into the sunset, and no one has to go to jail."

"Jail wasn't what I had in mind for you." Kaiah pulled out a gun and aimed it at Monroe, but he was too quick.

Monroe pulled Leo in front of himself and Kaiah's bullet hit the crewman instead. Monroe used the leverage of Leo falling to apprehend his pistol and turned it on Kaiah.

Instead of going for a kill, Monroe shot Kaiah's right arm, knocking his gun away and causing him to scream in pain.

Teagan, the crew leader, bent down and picked up the gun and trained it on Kaiah.

Within seconds, every other man in the room had a gun pointing at someone else. They were at a standoff. Whoever shot first would be the next to fall.

"Machudo," Monroe ordered the young man, "take the girls up on deck, and get them to safety."

None of the men moved a muscle to stop them as the girls cried with terror and followed Machudo.

"Now what?" Teagan asked, his voice containing nearly as much fear as the girls'.

"You tell me," Monroe said. "This is your ship."

"It's not my ship," Teagan said. "It's the captain's ship."

"Actually, this is my ship," Kaiah said, still doubled over in pain. "I am the legal owner." He clutched his right arm with his left. Blood seeped through his shirt.

"You are?" Teagan and several other men in the room asked simultaneously.

"My shell company is, yes." Kaiah somehow managed to sound cocky with pride even as he grew weak from blood loss.

How badly Monroe wanted to erase that smirk from his face.

"Hey, cuz." Henry nudged Monroe's shoulder. "How about if you and I follow Machudo and let these guys get back to their little party?"

"You're not going anywhere," Kaiah said. As if he had a choice. He was no longer armed and whichever of his cronies shot at Monroe would be shot instantly by either Henry or Teagan, possibly both. They would be stupid to shoot first even if Kaiah ordered him to. "You have been causing me problems since you dropped out of the sky yesterday."

"Wait, these are the guys who stole our prisoners?" one of Kaiah's men asked, anger rising in his voice.

"Who stole whom?" Monroe couldn't believe what he'd just heard.

"You just cost me twenty-three thousand dollars," the man said. He trained his gun on Monroe and fired.

Before Monroe hit the floor, two more gunshots rang in the small lounge. The man who shot Monroe met his demise.

The other body that fell was Kaiah Amali.

As he lay on the floor, Monroe was in so much pain he couldn't even figure out where he'd been shot. The last thing he remembered was Henry telling him to stay awake.

He didn't.

Epilogue: Take This Job
Army Captain Henry Stephenson

Monroe had saved Henry's life when he leapt from an airplane and landed in a campsite inhabited by kidnappers and child traffickers.

Now was the time for Henry to return the favor. He carried his cousin, bleeding and unconscious, from the belly of a freighter to the deck where chaos swirled around him.

There were so many uniformed soldiers, local law enforcement officers, Freedom Warriors, and crewmen from the ship that Henry couldn't tell who was friend or who was foe. Girls were crying, multiple people called out instructions to each other. None of pandemonium made sense and all Henry could think about was getting Monroe to a hospital.

The first bullet hit the Kevlar armor protecting Monroe's body. The second bullet was a little higher and grazed his neck, dangerously close to his spinal column. He was lucky that Henry hit the shooter just as the shooter got off the second round. The momentum changed the trajectory of the bullet, or it would have hit Monroe's head.

"Monroe!" A woman's voice called, and Henry turned to see the blonde intelligence analyst, Lieutenant Brianna Turner, from Monroe's company. She practically shoved Henry aside as she dropped to her knees near Monroe's head. "Is he going to be okay?"

Henry realized Lieutenant Turner had frantic tears running down her face and reality connected dots in his mind. She was in love with Monroe. No doubt he was in love with her also. Henry wished he could wake his cousin and ask him. "He's losing blood fast. We need to get him to a hospital."

Xavier rushed forward in answer to Henry's request. "We've already called for ambulances, but let's get him off the ship and onto the pier."

Monroe was a large man and dead weight. Four men from the Freedom Warriors group helped carry him down from the ship and they laid him on the pier.

Soon sirens howled in the distance and drew closer and closer.

"Hold on, buddy, they're coming to help," Henry said, as if Monroe could hear him. Maybe he could. Their cousin, Alex, had claimed to have seen and heard things while he was unconscious. Perhaps Monroe could as well. Henry clasped Monroe's hand in his and said again, "Hold on. Help is on its way."

Multiple ambulances sped down the pier and the guys helped Monroe into an ambulance. Lieutenant Turner climbed into the ambulance with him, and they sped away, taking one weight off Henry's shoulders.

Monroe leaving meant Henry was on his own. Except that he wasn't. Whitney from the Freedom Warriors hurried forward and threw herself into Henry's arms.

"I was so worried about you." She pulled back and looked him up and down. "Are you okay? Were you hurt? You're covered in blood."

"I'm fine," Henry said, pulling Whitney back into his arms. "The blood was from my cousin, Monroe. He was shot twice. He just left in that ambulance. Are you okay? Did the girls get to safety?" Henry nodded his head in the direction of the retreating ambulance.

"Yes, we have a team of aftercare workers helping get these girls to a safe house." Whitney's eyes were baggy and her hair was falling out of its sloppy bun.

"You're a miracle worker, you know that?" Henry said with pride.

"Just doing my job, Captain." Whitney patted him on the chest. "You know, we could use another strong guy, and you seem to be pretty good at this. You should join us."

"Considering I'll probably be decommissioned when I return to the States, I'll think about it," Henry said, kissing Whitney on the top of her head. "For now, we need to reinstate Prime Minister Nehemiah Paton to his position of power in the Belize government and get the Mayan girls back to their mothers."

The job wasn't over just because they freed the girls. Hopefully interrogations of the remaining kidnappers would provide more takedowns.

Yeah, Henry could visualize himself part of this team. He could make a real difference. It wouldn't hurt to look into. If he wasn't court marshalled for insubordination.

Time would tell. Henry was thankful to have something to fall back on when he lost his commission. His time in The National Guard was important. But helping Operation Freedom Warriors could really make a difference.

Plus, there was the added bonus of working everyday with Whitney. Henry threw his arm around Whitney's shoulders and led her away. "Let's return some girls to their families, shall we?"

"Sounds like a plan," Whitney said with a tired smile. With arms around each other's waists, Henry and Whitney strode over to find the others.

One week later...

"Heard they're finally gonna let you outa this hospital," Henry said to his cousin, gripping Monroe in a half hug and patting him on the shoulder. "You look good for a guy who almost died last week."

"I'm alive thanks to you," Monroe said, returning the hug.

"Right back at ya," Henry said, pulling up a chair. "Sometimes good deeds get rewarded."

"Yeah, well, neither of our good deeds kept us from being dishonorably discharged." Monroe rolled his eyes and swore under his breath. "That's what we get for being heroes."

"I'd do it again in a heartbeat, man," Henry said. "You would too, and you know it."

"Yeah, but I want to be able to..." Monroe's voice trailed off, and he looked away. "Why'd this have to happen to me, man? I was trying to help those girls. Shouldn't that count for something?"

"You *did* help those girls," Henry said. "Between the girls on the reservation and the girls in the warehouse, you helped liberate sixty-five kidnapped girls from a life of trafficking."

"Yeah, I'm a real hero." Monroe's statement was laced with sarcasm. "I'm gonna be decommissioned. I'll never jump out of an airplane again. I'll never kick down a door to rescue the person on the other side. I'm worthless."

"Listen to me," Henry said. "A hero is not the guy who jumps from the plane or kicks in the door. A hero is the person who does what he can in his corner of the world. There is still work to be done, and you can play a part in that work as soon as you get your head out of your rear end and stop feeling sorry for yourself."

"I just wish I would have handled things differently and maybe I could have kept my job."

"You could take Xavier up on his offer to come work with us at Operation Freedom Warriors. We're making a difference in the lives of kids caught up in child sex trafficking. We need special ops guys like you."

"You've got Aaron's money," Monroe said. "You can hire somebody."

"We want to hire you," Henry said. "Don't get me wrong, we really appreciate Aaron's money. Without donors, we wouldn't be able to keep doing what we're doing. Even a little donation can help, but a major donor like him is rare."

"If I was a billionaire, I'd give lots of money," Monroe said. "But I'm not."

"But you have specialized skills that few people have. I want you to go through the free training on their website. Even just becoming informed about the signs of human trafficking is a great first step. Then, if you still want to find some other job, I'll respect that. This line of work isn't for everyone. But if you do want to get involved, we can put you to good use right away."

"You sound like a walking commercial," Monroe said. "You've officially been with the organization, what? A day and a half?"

"A week," Henry said. "You were pretty out of it those first few days after surgery."

"Fine, I'll do the free training on their website," Monroe said. "But I'm not making any promises beyond that."

Just then, Brianna walked into Monroe's hospital room, and his face lit up. "Good afternoon, Lieutenant."

"Good afternoon, Captain." Brianna leaned down and kissed Monroe.

"And that's my cue to leave," Henry said with a chuckle. He couldn't fault the love birds for wanting to make out a little. Henry offered his cousin one last fist bump, gave Brianna a quick hug, and then headed home to Whitney, excited to start this next phase in his life.

<u>Continue reading the Royal Family Saga – Book Three: Billionaire Professors (The Geek Twins)</u>

Operation Underground Railroad

I almost feel as if I need quotation marks around certain portions of this story because they so closely resemble the words of Tim Ballard, founder of Operation Underground Railroad (O.U.R.).

Everything that Xavier Fulton says is almost word-for-word a conglomerate of how Tim would tell the story. I've watched so many speeches Tim has given it would be nearly impossible to separate out his words from my own creative and artistic liberty in telling the story of Operation Underground Railroad. Interviews, presentations, anything he has posted on his website and YouTube channel, I've watched it. So, I'm just going to credit anything that Xavier says in this story to Tim. Tim Ballard, this story is for you.

I also plan to donate a portion of the proceeds from the sale of this book to Operation Underground Railroad (O.U.R.), the organization around which I pattered Operation Freedom Warriors in my book. I first learned about O.U.R. from a critique partner of mine, Shannon Symonds, who encouraged me to participate in Authors for Freedom in the summer of 2020. I was so touched by this organization I ended up donating more than the proceeds from my sales on the day of the promotion. I told my husband that we need to do more. He agreed and said, yes, write the check.

When I wrote this book, I knew we needed to do even more. I can only do what I can do. You can only do what you can do. But together our little bits add up to more. We can do more. Thank you for purchasing this book. Just in doing that one little thing, you have contributed. I hope you loved the story and that you'll continue reading the Royal Family Saga.

Sincerely, Julie L. Spencer

Learn more about Operation Underground Railroad (O.U.R.)

Billionaire Professors (The Geek Twins)

Continue reading the Royal Family Saga – Book Three: Billionaire Professors (The Geek Twins)

Twin geeky brothers, two sweet romance love stories, and one treasure hunt in the jungles of Guatemala.

Dr. Nicholas Stephenson, a Harvard professor of archaeology, and his twin brother, Dr. Levi Stephenson, a professor of linguistics, are lured away from their ivory tower to embark on a treasure hunt.

Nick's college crush, the sultry and flirtatious Dr. Rebecca Benson is an expert at airborne laser mapping, and Nick can't say no to helping her when she discovers a secret that rewrites history.

In the jungles of Guatemala, the team of scientists stumbles upon a tribe of Mayans determined to stop the scientists from reaching their sacred pyramid. Only through Levi's ability to communicate with the haughty and elegant daughter of the tribal chief, Tiani Sayid, are they able to convince the tribal warriors to step down and lower their spears.

But at what price?

Continue reading the Royal Family Saga – Book Three: Billionaire Professors (The Geek Twins)

Acknowledgments

Lisa Rector, I could never thank you enough for your editing skills. You truly save me time and again from publishing stories with huge, gaping holes, and commas in all the wrong places.

Thanks, Brenda Walter for another fabulous cover design. You outdo yourself over and over.

Audrianna Anderson, thank you for being my right-hand woman, administrative assistant, personal assistant, virtual assistant, social media coordinator, sounding board, cheerleader, sometimes-counselor, and true f riend.

Shannon Symonds, thanks for introducing me to Authors for Freedom and Operation Underground Railroad. You know, I'd get more sleep if you and I lived in the same time zone!

Thank you, Lara Wynter, for reading my books from the other side of the world and telling me how this story would be different if told from Australia. Also, for helping me fix some things to be more understandable for my international readers. Let's rock!

To my Chapter-A-Day super fans, particularly Joel Rees, Laura Palmer, Paula Hurdle, Bonnie Congrove-Fritz, Teya Peck, Julie Berryman, Lori Smith, Sally Pomerantz, and Crissy Holland. You give me a reason to write every day and fix my mistakes on the fly.

Most especially, thank you to God and to my husband, children, and family. You are my inspiration.

-Julie L. Spencer

About Author Julie Spencer

Julie is a bestselling multi-genre author who writes under three pen names. Her young adult sports romance have a little less spice and little more sweet-n-innocent. As Julie Spencer and Julie L. Spencer, she writes books with more serious subjects and maybe some religion thrown in.

Her more controversial books can be found under the new pen name J.L. Spencer. These books come with a content warning and may contain a little more heat, spice, and perhaps a few discussions about or trips to the main characters' bedrooms.

All of her stories include snarky, flawed characters, and romantic twists and turns. Julie believes we can change the world one story at a time.

www.AuthorJulieSpencer.com

All's Fair in Love and Sports Series

Take Me to the Winter Games

Meet Me at the Summer Games

Ride the Halfpipe with Me

Pass Me the Ball

Catching Waves with You

<u>Strike Three, You're Mine</u>

<u>Meet Me at Half Court</u>

<u>Cheer for Me</u>

<u>Basketballs and Mistletoe</u>

<u>Running to You</u>

<u>Matching You with Love</u>
(with co-author Audi Lynn Anderson)

<u>All's Fair in Love and Sports Collection</u>

<u>Prince of Israel Series on Kindle Vella</u>

<u>First Prince of Israel</u>

<u>(Prequel to the Prince of Israel Series)</u>

Royal Family Saga Series

<u>Billionaire Crown Prince</u>

<u>Billionaire Hero</u>

Billionaire Professors (The Geek Twins)

Billionaire's Brother

Billionaire's Sons

Honorary Prince

Royal Family Saga Special Editions

Royal Family Saga Volume I

Royal Family Saga Volume II

Royal Family Saga Volume III

Love Letters Series

Who Wants to Marry a Mormon Girl?

Who Wants to Marry a Billionaire Gamer?

Christian Romance

The Cove

The Farmer's Daughter

The Man in the Yellow Jaguar

The Refusal

Rock Star Redemption Series

Almost a Rock Star

Billionaire Rock Star

International Rock Star

Fallen Rock Star

Forever a Rock Star

Rock Star Redemption Series – Complete Collection

Opening Act: Buxton Peak Meets Infusion Deep

Opening Act: Infusion Deep Meets Buxton Peak
(with co-author Lara Wynter)

Julie writes some more controversial books under the pen name J.L. Spencer

These books may contain heat, spice, and perhaps a few discussions about or trips to the main characters' bedrooms.

Here is a list if you'd like to check them out:

Road Trip

Combustion

A Million Bucks

Hidden Swan

She's Not My Sister

Nonfiction

Writing Romance Is Not About Sex… or Is It? How Far Is Too Far in Clean Romance?

How to Outline a Romance Novel – Fiction Writing Skills for Romance Authors

How to Write a Romantic Subplot – How to Add Romance to Other Plot Structures

Listen to audiobooks by Julie L. Spencer

All's Fair in Love and Sports Series

<u>Running to You</u>

<u>Meet Me at Half Court</u>

<u>Pass Me the Ball</u>

<u>Basketballs and Mistletoe</u>

<u>Strike Three, You're Mine</u>

Social Issues

<u>Combustion</u>

Royal Family Saga

<u>Billionaire Crown Prince</u>

Billionaire Hero

Love Letters Series

Who Wants to Marry a Mormon Girl?

Who Wants to Marry a Billionaire Gamer?

Rock Star Redemption Series

Almost a Rock Star

Billionaire Rock Star

International Rock Star

Fallen Rock Star

Forever a Rock Star

Rock Star Redemption Series Complete Collection

Christian Romance

<u>The Cove</u>

<u>The Man in the Yellow Jaguar</u>

www.ingramcontent.com/pod-product-compliance
Lightning Source LLC
Chambersburg PA
CBHW071331250626
47159CB00004B/1561